CREATIVE WRITING FROM NORTH AND EAST LONDON

Edited by Heather Killingray

First published in Great Britain in 2002 by
YOUNG WRITERS
Remus House,
Coltsfoot Drive,
Peterborough, PE2 9JX
Telephone (01733) 890066

HB ISBN 0 75432 718 3
SB ISBN 0 75432 719 1

FOREWORD

This year Young Writers proudly presents a showcase of the best 'Days Of Our Lives . . .' short stories, from up-and-coming writers nationwide.

To write a short story is a difficult exercise. We made it more challenging by setting the theme of 'A Day In The Life Of Someone From The Second Millennium', using no more than 250 words! Much imagination and skill is required. *Days Of Our Lives . . . Creative Writing From North & East London* achieves and exceeds these requirements. This exciting anthology will not disappoint the reader.

The thought, effort, imagination and hard work put into each story impressed us all, and again, the task of editing proved demanding due to the quality of entries received, but was nevertheless enjoyable.

We hope you are as pleased as we are with the final selection and that you continue to enjoy *Days Of Our Lives . . . Creative Writing From North & East London* for many years to come.

CONTENTS

St John Vianney RC Primary School

The Stories

A DAY IN THE LIFE OF JACQUELINE WILSON!

Hi, I'm Jacqueline Wilson and I'm a very famous author. I'm famous for writing comedy stories and Nick Sharatt illustrates for all my books! I've written quite a lot of stories like Girls In Love, Girls Under Pressure and Girls Out Late! They come in a series about three girls who have problems in the beginning but in the end turn out fine as they are! I've written stories for younger children and lots for older children! I'm planning to write more stories for older children and make another series about girls. I'd like to learn how to draw like Nick Sharatt! He draws these really awesome pictures!

I'd like to do something else in my life apart from writing stories all day long. Something really enjoyable, something that other people like to do. Or maybe do something to involve children who don't like to read. Well, I'll carry on with my stories now!

Layla Ebrahim-Khan (10)
Barrow Hill Junior School

A Day In The Life Of An Ant

A terrible sight of a giant monster. What could it be? A table, chair, car, TV, bed, human *ting ting!* Yes I got it, a human. Huge and repulsive, what else can I say. Killing us is bad behaviour.

Look at us down there we lay. We need revenge but how? We are too tiny for the giant monsters. I guess there's only one way, to take the mickey down all this way. Look at them - two eyes, two hands, two ears, two feet, clothes and trainers. How do they ever survive in the heat?

It comes to night. I scurry up to a dirty old tramp that is snoring away beside the Queen Vic. Boy he smells! He smells so awful that I have nothing left to do for the day. Well I guess that's the end of my day. What a scruffy day ants have in their lives.

Samad Ahmed (10)
Barrow Hill Junior School

A DAY IN THE LIFE OF MANDY GREY

I was stuck. Alone in a damp mossy castle. I was being wrapped up in the cold night air.

I lay down on the ice cold floor wishing for just one piece of cloth to keep me warm. Then I noticed the shape of a door in the stone wall, but there was no handle. The rough stones sticking out. I thought this was an old castle. Maybe if I pushed a stone it would open. I got up steadily and walked over to the wall like a mouse coming out from hiding. My arm brushed a stone viciously leaving scratches brimming with blood. I pushed a stone. The door spun round instantly on its side. I walked in. Light filled a narrow passage. Figures of light danced on the walls. As I went deeper into the passage. I felt like I was going downhill. The passage formed a joyful chamber filled with mouth-watering foods of all sorts. As I walked over to the table I fell through a deep hole. I landed on the ground hurting my back painfully.

Then I woke up, my face dripping with sweat.

The smell of food swept into my bedroom. I got dressed then hurried downstairs for my mum's special Saturday fry up breakfast.

Louise Rabin (10)
Barrow Hill Junior School

A Day In The Life Of An Alien From . . .

The planet that I come from is as red as blood. There are lots of rivers too.

Some earthlings refer to me as hideous, slimy and imaginary. Well they're the ones that are ugly if you ask me, to be honest they're pretty stupid too. They trespass on *our* land and expect to find us, but guess what? They're too stupid to even do that! Ha! Typical right! And they don't even have the respect to name us after something important rather than chocolate bars!

As you have guessed I am from the planet *Mars!* We invented flying saucers and spaceships, we do have schools in Mars not like earthlings' schools we actually *learn* something!

The other day we visited our relatives on Jupiter and Saturn, Pluto and Venus!

Zainab Al-Farabi (10)
Barrow Hill Junior School

A Day In The Life Of The Monster At The Bottom Of The Sea

In the immense depth of the Pacific Ocean, 3194 miles below the surface, a dreary shape cast over the gravel at the bottom of the sea, sleeping soundly was the master of three: an undisturbed figure just waiting to awake. Suddenly a slight movement predicted that the huge creature would soon be awake . . . Whoosh, a few seconds later the greatly powerful beast swiped viciously and tore to little shreds a fully-grown hammerhead shark only one sixth of its size! The blood-stained water swayed back and forth as if it was trying to knock out the monster. The half fish half bird creature was gaining tremendous speed! It was as agile as a mouse, but as great as a dinosaur . . . Then it bellowed; in its speed it crashed through the barrier in which water and air were separated and flew into the night sky. It passed the moon and stars as if it were in space; it travelled across the world, past *all* the continents and finally to the glittering moon and back! As the amazing creature dived into the ocean once again it became morning and the glowing orange sun came out. Then some other strange multi-coloured creature appeared . . . but this one had a rainbow trailing it . . . Then it disappeared.

Robert Allan (10)
Barrow Hill Junior School

A Day In The Life Of A Dolphin

Splish! Splash! Splush! My fins feel as if they're taking me where I want to go. Rushing viciously through the water, pushing everything aside. They are the monsters of the deep, they are in control of me, and I must obey for I have no choice. The water surrounds me in a deep blue blanket I can't get out of. I zoom up to the surface like a rocket blasting off for the moon at full speed. I reach the surface and dive above the water, and as the deep blueness comes back into weary view and painfully stings my face as if spikes were being pushed into me, I think to myself I used to do this with my friends! Friends that have been so unfairly, so, so, unfairly caught in nets. Or at least that's what I think they are! You do this, you know you do. I'm a survivor, one of the only ones. That doesn't mean that me and the other survivors are not scared. We are terrified.

My fins fearfully slow down, I hardly even glide through the water. It creates a ticklish wave piercing my skin. My rough, blue, scaly skin pushed past the water gently.

But then I remember . . .

It's up to you. You can save me, plus thousands of other dolphins. There can be more of me, but it's up to you. You can help. You know you can. There could be hundreds of us . . . thousands . . . millions . . . *billions!*

Joanna Brecher (10)
Barrow Hill Junior School

A Day In The Life Of A Tyrannosaurus Rex

Hi, I'm Tyrannosaurus Rex, but call me Rex for short. Did you know, I'm the coolest, bravest, toughest and fiercest Tyrannosaurus Rex in the world? Well now you know.

Now today you're going to spend a day with me to see all the cool moves I do. Mmmm, mmmm. Mighty fine!

Oh, look. There's a lovely Pterodactyl for my lunch. Oh God, this is a really tough job to do because if I move or stamp it's like there's an earthquake. Then I can't sneak up on them.

Even though I'm a pretty big animal, I could easily get this measly puny Pterodactyl.

Munch, munch, crunch, crunch, gobble, gobble! That was lovely! I've just had something to eat but I'm still hungry. Well, I could maybe eat you but then? *Nah!*

Excuse me a minute. I just need to wipe my mouth. Wipe, wipe. Sorry about that. It is because I know you humans get a little squeamish when you see blood.

Well, let's not waste time. Now, I'm going to teach you how to kill prey. Now the first step is to creep up. The second, you have to get real close to your prey, and last of all - catch and *crunch!*

Well, I hope you enjoyed your brilliant, splendid, amazing, extraordinary time here! I hope to see you again! Bye!

Eloisa Henderson-Figueroa (10)
Barrow Hill Junior School

A DAY IN THE LIFE OF ENID BLYTON

Hi, I'm Enid Blyton!

I wrote The Famous Five, The Secret Seven, Noddy and lots more!

Today is my birthday! Come share the day with me. What shall we do first! Hmmmm, let's have breakfast.

I started a new book yesterday. It's called 'A Day In The Life Of Enid Blyton'.

I received an invitation from my best friend Joanne Rowling, who lives next-door. I'm sure you know her. She writes Harry Potter books. I love them!

Let's go visit her!
'Hello Joanne.'
'Hello Enid,' Joanne says.
I go inside down the hall and 'surprise' all the authors in England are in her hall! 'This is amazing, *wow!'* I turn around . . . behind me is a tall pile of . . . *presents!* I haven't had that many since I was eleven! I look at everyone and they shout 'Happy Birthday!' On a table there is a birthday cake shaped as a book with 'Happy Birthday Enid' written across it. I've not had a cake this wonderful since I was a kid! Everyone starts singing, I blow the candles and make my wish! Everyone claps and I'm happy. I have some cake. It's heavenly! It's time to open my presents. They are lovely; I have books, clothes and all sorts of things! Then, sadly the party is over.

I leave happily and go home. *Aaahhh* I'm exhausted. I hope you enjoyed the day, I certainly did!

I hope you come again! Bye!

Love Enid Blyton

Trinita Attanayave (9)
Barrow Hill Junior School

A Day In The Life Of France

On Thursday it was France V Portugal. France started the kick off, and in a few minutes France had the ball near Portugal's goal, when France passed it to Wiltord and it's a *goal!* Lazio, France scored 1-0, a wonderful pass to Wiltord and he shot it perfectly in the goal. 1-0 to France, then France got it again, this time it's Henry. What a run. Then Henry nearly got tackled but kicks a cross in. Going into the goal, yes *goal!* Lazio, right in the low right-hand corner of the goal. 2-0 to France and now it's half time.

It's the second half. Portugal start the kick off after a few minutes. France got the ball. He's running to the goal, a lovely cross *it's in! Goal!* Lazio, what a goal by France. The French supporters are wild 3-0 to France. France are really confident about winning this match and to beat Portugal badly and a wonderful goal kick by Portugal and a wonderful header by France. After a few minutes France got the ball again right near the goal and it's a *goal!* Lazio 4-0 to France, France are in the lead with 4-0. No change for Portugal. The second half is over. France has won the match.

What a match for France, France played really well. Good skill on the pitch and defending well. I hope next time they play Portugal, Portugal will maybe win.

William De Souza Tigre (9)
Barrow Hill Junior School

A Day In The Life Of Harriet Tubman, Freedom Fighter

We had to get up early so we could get going. I'd just heard that Charles Nalle was being held prisoner in Troy. I was going to organise a rescue party.

We got going pretty quickly because Charles Nalle was going to be taken to court the next day.

It took a whole twenty miles to get to Troy; we stopped at a station to rest, but not for long because we had to keep going. One time Crala (that's one of the people I rescued) wanted to turn back but I threatened her with my gun and she kept going.

We got to Troy about eight o'clock in the evening. I was really tired but I still found out where Charles Nalle was imprisoned. It took a long time to find enough people for a rescue. At ten to twelve we set out to find the prison. We had to get to work quickly.

When we got Charles Nalle out he was so hungry, thirsty and tired, that we had to stop at a place where I had stopped before. An old lady lived in that place. We went to bed feeling tired but not hungry. We will have a long day tomorrow.

Alice White (9)
Barrow Hill Junior School

A Day In The Life Of Tracy Beaker!

Today I just gulped down my breakfast and stuffed my bag with stuff and shouted 'Goodbye Cam!' but before she could answer I had slammed the door shut. I decided to bunk off school today. I've had enough of school and Mrs VB (Mrs Vomit Bagley!).

A couple of days ago Mrs VB told us to do this family tree sheet and I said that my mum was a Hollywood star and that she was in films and couldn't come to see me because she was so busy. Mrs VB embarrassed me so much that I nearly started to get my hay fever back again.

So I was running down the street, it looked like my house and I opened the front door and I saw the house looked much tidier than before, and there was a bowl of Smarties all set out smart. I heard a little sneeze behind the curtains, it was a boy and I shouted
'What are you doing in my house, who are you?'
'I-I-I'm Tracy Beaker!' I said proudly. So we kept talking about stuff and I stayed there for the rest of the day. I finally decided to go back to my 'real' home.

When I got back Cam gave me this long lecture about not bunking off school and other stuff. Finally I gave up and went to bed, saying 'Yeah, yeah!'

Charlotte Priestley (9)
Barrow Hill Junior School

A DAY IN THE LIFE OF CHRIS TUCKER

Morning:

In the morning I woke up at 6am. This is because I had to eat my breakfast before 6.30am. I had a film rehearsal. My film now is called 'Rush Hour' I'm acting with a very popular martial arts person, Jackie Chan. I can't wait.

I felt so nervous. When it was time to do the rehearsal I had to get a stuntman to do the dangerous actions, for instance, jumping off a 24-storey building. The rehearsal took five hours.

Afternoon:

When lunchtime came I had it in my dressing room. It was delicious. After that the film group called for a meeting about improvements. It took about half-an-hour. The director said that Jackie and I could use real guns that only shot blanks, to make it more real. I bought clothes that would suit parts of the film. Jackie bought a gun-holder. It was fun.

Evening:

In the evening I had dinner in a 7-star hotel. The food was Italian. I ordered three pizzas and two bowls of spaghetti. I was really hungry. I stayed in a room with a king-sized bed, and went to sleep . . .

Byron Morrell (9)
Barrow Hill Junior School

A DAY IN THE LIFE OF ARNOLD SCHWARZENEGGER!

Hey, I am Arnold Schwarzenegger and this is my ordinary life. I get up and brush my teeth so the girls will like me. Then I check out my enormous muscles. I get my bullet-proof jacket so I do not get hurt. Then I put on my red T-shirt, snake boots and black trousers and head off to work.

My work is acting and today I'm doing the role of a spy. First they give me a script and I read it, then I act it with the script. At lunch I go to a quiet restaurant so I can concentrate on my script and eat my lunch. It takes me five hours and twenty minutes. Then I do the acting without a script.

At dinner time I go to the pub and have a beer and then go to sleep. I dreamt I was a good actor.

Gloria Hawke (9)
Barrow Hill Junior School

A DAY IN THE LIFE OF SUGAR COLLETT

I had just come back from Kilburn when Nick came in with a large box in his hand. My mum thought it was a cat because it was that big. I got all excited.

I opened the box and there she was, a teeny weeny little hamster in its cage. My eyes popped and little love hearts flew down. There were a few little poos because she was scared. I picked her up and nearly smothered her until she tried to escape.
We called her Sugar.
I had just left Mum with Sugar when a scream came from the room she was in . . .
I ran in with my heart beating because I was so scared. Mum began to cry, I just burst out crying too because I didn't know what had happened to Sugar.
Mum tried to explain what went wrong, she said Sugar had escaped through a hole in our sofa. Nick and Mum searched around for a pair of scissors to cut open the sofa, it was the only thing that could be done. But what if something terrible happened to her? My eyes watered with big, fat, salty teardrops.
I couldn't watch.
Nick and Mum snapped the material covering the old sofa and put their hands into it.
'I've got her!' shouted Nick taking her out of the sofa. Nick carefully put Sugar in her cage and closed the door, while he did that he whispered,
'No more adventures today.'

Miranda Collett (9)
Barrow Hill Junior School

A DAY IN THE LIFE OF A DOLPHIN

A day in the life of a dolphin would be great fun, I would wake up, swim around and wait until someone came to feed me then when some people came to see me, because I lived in an aquarium, I would do tricks and children would touch my lovely smooth, grey skin.

I like it a lot when disabled adults and children visit me because I know I comfort them and amaze them and make them happy and they laugh.

Sometimes people get in and swim with me, it's great fun for them and for me, people do tricks like standing on my back or on my nose while I'm swimming.

I'm a really loveable animal and very affectionate. People love to play with me and I love to play. I love to swim around my pool and with my other dolphin friends. The people who own the aquarium are really nice but I have my own personal owner who just feeds me and looks after me. She is really nice and friendly. She's looked after me since I was born. She sometimes gets in and swims with me. I also do shows in front of hundreds and hundreds of people, it really excites me because everyone is watching me and clapping and cheering although sometimes I get nervous. I get a very special treat when I have training for shows and if I do well, at the end of the day when it starts to get dark, I have more food. It's delicious.

Then I go to sleep and have a nice long rest, ready for tomorrow. It's great being a dolphin but I have to admit it can sometimes get tiring.

Shelley Gosling (10)
Beaumont Primary School

A DAY IN THE LIFE OF MY MUM

Ring, ring! Oh no, it's the alarm clock! I hate that noise. It means time to get the boys up.

'Hello Lucy.'

'Miaow.'

'OK, I'll go and get your food. Wakey, wakey, rise and shine, get washed while I go and feed the cats and comb my hair because it's sticking up.'

'OK' said Liam and Saran.

So I went downstairs and gave the cats their food. Then I had my breakfast.

'Mum!' said Liam.

'Yes,' I said. I ran up and got the towels for them. 'Jump out then and pull the plug out.'

They got out and I said 'Get dry, then eat your breakfast, it's on the table.'

While they were getting dried and dressed, I got dressed. 'Where's that comb now, oh here.' Comb, comb. 'That looks better. Boys!'

'Yes?'

'Have you changed for school?'

'Yes.'

'Good. Get your gear and give me a kiss. Have you brushed your teeth?'

'Yes.'

'Right goodbye, be good!'

Now they've gone to school I get my shoes and get ready to go to work. I get into the lift and go down to the ground. It takes about two minutes to get there.

'Hello Kim. Hello Trevor. Hello Cath.'

They said 'You're working at the till until 3 o'clock.'

We made £60 by 12 o'clock. I had my lunch and got on with my work. At the end of the day we had made £90.

I then went to pick the children up.

'Can we go home?'

'Yes,' I said.

When we got home we watched a video and ate lovely chicken, rice and chips. The video was good. Afterwards I tucked them into bed after they had brushed their teeth and off they went to sleep.

Saran Golden (10)
Beaumont Primary School

A Day In The Life Of A Roman Soldier

I woke up and found myself in a cottage, a very dirty, old cottage. I had on a dirty, itchy shirt and very dirty trousers. I opened the door and went outside and asked a man, 'What year is this?'
He said 'The year is 117AD.'
I looked around and saw lots of mud and hens all around. All of a sudden I saw Roman soldiers knocking on people's houses.

I went back into my house and thought, 'What are Roman soldiers doing here, knocking on people's houses?' Oh no, this is the year when the Roman soldiers are going to fight the Barbarians. All of a sudden someone knocked on my door. I opened it. There were some Roman soldiers.

They said 'Join our army because we are fighting the Barbarians and there are not enough soldiers King Tarjan has said.'

I didn't know what to say so I wrote my name and joined the Roman army. They took me in their carriage. It was very hard training. I have heard that the Romans have four thousand nine hundred soldiers. I wondered which army would win. I hoped we would. It was our lesson time, the Roman Captain was telling us what to wear for the war. The Roman King Tarjan had a box with many names in. All the soldiers sat down and the King said in a loud voice 'In this box there are many excellent gladiators. If I pull a name from that box, that person will be a captain of 2000 men. King Tarjan picked a name out and said 'Asim.'
I stood up, the King gave me a golden gladiator sword. The captain of the Roman army came to me and said:
'The Barbarians are asking people as well to join their army.'

The battle began, I had taken my army to a field. The captain said 'Charge' and the soldiers ran down. The captain said 'Where are all the Barbarians?'

The Barbarians were in the trees. They jumped on the Romans' back and started stabbing them. There was fire everywhere. The three captains were with me as well as King Tarjan. We all charged into the forest but the Barbarians weren't there. They jumped on the Roman calvery. The Roman soldiers turned into turtles and put their spears out.

The Barbarians were stuck. And the Romans charged. It was a sick and bloody battle. The Barbarians' king ran, I charged after him, I pushed him on the floor and stabbed him. The Romans went back to the palace. In front of King Tarjan the Barbarians dropped their weapons. I was the best General in the world.

All of a sudden something happened, everything started to vanish. Bang! I woke up and it was all a dream. Oh no, it's my test in history and what happened in 117AD. I just went through 117AD so I know everything that happened.

Asim Mohammed (10)
Beaumont Primary School

A DAY IN THE LIFE OF AMANDA OBRA

It's a Sunday morning, I wake up at 6.45am. As usual I am tired and grumpy. My family has breakfast. It's actually a short breakfast due to having to rush to church so my mum can be in time to do a reading for 'Father Jim'. My dad drops the family to church before he goes bowling with some friends. He does that every Sunday.

After Mass, my mum sometimes takes time to light a candle. While she does that, my younger sister aged nine goes out to buy sweets. 'It's a waste of money!' says my older sister aged fourteen.

We walk home. Once we get home, we have a proper breakfast. My mum tells me to revise some books for the next day, it is my SATs. During revising, I listen to my CD player to keep me going.

The following day, (which is Monday) the same things happen; I wake up at 6.45am . . . have breakfast . . . etc. My older sister leaves the house for secondary school, it takes her twenty minutes to get there.

My dad drops us off at school. Day after day, I cross the 'zebra crossing' with my younger sister and enter the gates to school. I always ask my sister if she can see any of my friends since I am short-sighted. Then I walk up to them and talk till Miss Newman rings the bell. Waiting outside the classroom is my teacher telling us to hurry up. Once my SATs started, I thought to myself it was easier than I expected!

Amanda Obra (11)
Blessed Sacrament RC Primary School

UNTITLED

I was finally there, front row seat, fifteen rounds of boxing, Mohammed Ali vs Sonny Liston. Sonny Liston was in the ring waiting for his opponent. At that moment heading for the ring was the greatest, Mohammed Ali, he stepped through the ring very focused.

'Ladies and gentlemen the next bout will be for the world championships,' the ring announcer informed us. 'In the blue corner with the height of five foot eight and weighing ninety-six pounds, Sonny Liston and in the red corner at six foot four and ninety pounds, the greatest the world champion, Mohammed Ali.'

Ding, ding the bell rang. The two fighters moved around the ring. The champion was dancing about hitting the left jab in the eye. Liston moved in and landed a body shot and pushed Ali in the corner, Ali fell but the bell rang.

For every round Ali was getting better. Suddenly off the rope with lightning speed was Ali who knocked Liston out cold.

James O'Neill (11)
Blessed Sacrament RC Primary School

A DAY AT SCHOOL

One morning I wake up and my mum makes me have some breakfast and wash my face and hands and then go to school. First, my teacher does the register then Robert and Juliana take it down. Then we all line up in assembly order and go down. After assembly, some children go down to Class 8 to do some maths. At 10.30 we have break then we come in and do some more maths. Then we do some English grammar for about one hour, then the lunch bell goes and we go out for lunch. One of the dinner ladies rings the bell and takes a class in. At last Year 6 goes in and there is not a lot of food to eat because of the other classes.

When we've finished, we go out to play, there are not a lot of things to do because we are having our playground done. So we have to play with the lunchtime things. They are all so boring. Then the toilet bell goes and everyone goes to the loo. 5 minutes later we have to go in. Then we do science or religion all afternoon. Then the bell goes again and we pack up and go home.

Sean Pullen (11)
Blessed Sacrament RC Primary School

A Day In The Life Of Jamaal Vital

I wake up quite early, tired and groggy. As the day goes on I feel better. I have toast with butter and a drink of orange juice. I wear my full school uniform and a ring on my finger, but the school headteacher recently told us that no rings are allowed. I go and I read for a while, revising before having my SATs.

To get in the school, there is a security lock in the main door in which I have to enter four numbers which only the headteacher and the other teachers know, but above, there is a button that I must press then someone will be on-line. They will ask you who you are, just to make sure.

What is it about school that makes it so interesting? It's the learning and teaching. Schools can be interesting but disciplined. Certain teachers do not usually work in the school, therefore, they are supply teachers. They mainly come from South America, Australia and Jamaica. The funniest supply teacher, which is my opinion but not just mine, comes from Jamaica.

Anyway I find the SATs quite hard, but alright. Also we are asked if we would like higher grade work which is hard but good to learn.

Jamaal Vital (11)
Blessed Sacrament RC Primary School

A DAY IN THE LIFE OF A LIZARD

My lizard is a Leopard Gecko. It can grow up to nine or twelve inches long including the tail. When I bought it, it was about three inches long but after having it for four months, it has grown to seven inches long.

What I have to feed it is disgusting, we have to feed it live crickets. We buy them in box which we put in the cage and let them out. If we don't let them out, then the lizard jumps in.

My lizard seemed lonely so I bought another one so it won't feel lonely. They seem to get along so I have to buy double the amount of crickets. They can be fed by hand, but what is worse than crickets? Dead baby mice! My lizard's friend is about 5½ inches long, sometimes they have arguments as to who gets to sleep in the cave. One sleeps on the sunning rock all day so it's hot to eat at night because they are cold-blooded. I need to get a bigger cage because there are two and they are getting bigger.

Alfie Carr (11)
Blessed Sacrament RC Primary School

A Day In The Life Of Jesus

I am sleeping very happily until my mum wakes me up, 'Get up, sleeping beauty, there's a bowl of porridge and a vitamin on the table, have a wash and brush your teeth' (she's always moaning). I get my stuff ready for school, say goodbye and walk out very unhappily. I meet up with my friends at school, and we have a laugh, but *ring, ring!* The bell goes, we all go quiet as we go up to the classroom.

We take the boring register, then we go to uninteresting assembly. We come back and do never-ending maths. We go to break from half-ten to quarter to eleven, it can be good but it can be rubbish. We go in and do English for one and a half hours (it is so annoying). Then we go to lunch, we stay out until 1.30, when we come in and do science for the rest of the afternoon. Then we get our stuff to go home, after that we say five Hail Marys, one Glory Be and one Our Father, then we leave the room one after another. My friends and I talk about how we don't like school.

Children would be surprised if they could hear the other teachers and me talking in the staffroom. That's right, I'm a teacher!

Jessica Brady (10)
Blessed Sacrament RC Primary School

A Day In The Life Of Martin Luther King

The sun shines brightly through my bedroom window as I wake up. I hear my wife singing sweetly as I make my way to the bathroom. There I have a wash and brush my teeth. As I leave the bathroom, I see a queue of little heads waiting to brush their teeth.

Changing into my priest's uniform, I set off down the stairs where my wife is serving out our breakfast, kissing her, I sit down. My children come running down in the nightwear ready for breakfast. We all sit down, say Grace and eat our breakfast.

The children go upstairs to get ready for church and my wife and I clear away the breakfast things. When we are all ready for church we set off. The church, as usual, is covered in racist signs saying *'Coloured Only'* and *'Leave Blacks!'* Our church, like everything else in this country, is for Blacks only.

We enter the church and I take the stand, it is time for my early morning service, we start the day with Our Father and then I give my service. The point of my service is to emphasise the hope that one day black and white people can walk hand-in-hand as siblings and to achieve this goal using non-violent methods.

When I have finished my service we go home to find a flaming cross in our front porch. I cannot believe anyone would stoop so low. Thinking I will give in they have performed this shameful act but the lives of many Blacks are in my hands and I can't let them die even if I have to die for it . . .

Vaitehi Nageshwaran (11)
Forest Girls' School

A Day In The Lfe Of Suzanne From Hear'say

'Hi, I am Suzanne from Hear'say and this is our song *Pure and Simple.*'
I'm doing an early show today. I don't know why, seeing as no one gets
up

> 'I know I've been waking around in a dazey baby, baby'

at five o'clock unless they really

> 'Pure and simple going a be there'

have to.

'So Suzanne, how would you like to inspire people?'
'Well, first of all, I hope I inspire people to keep on at their dreams and
secondly, to think and be positive and confident about achieving them.'

It's the end of the show so let's have some fun. I'm going to chat to the
rest of the group and get something to eat.
We need to practise our songs and dance routines now.

'Ow! Ow! That's my foot Danny!'
'Sorry, sorry, I am so sorry, I really did not mean to do that.'
'I know you didn't mean to. I'll just go and sit down for a while.'
'Ow, that really hurts. I think I've broken a toe. Hmmm, no, I can move
it. I'm just going to get a drink you guys.'

Danny, so nice, but so clumsy.
Kym, sensitive and wild.
Noel funny, with smelly feet.
Myleene, sensible with a great sense of humour.

Ahh, nothing beats a pleasant drink when you're thirsty, I feel much
better now. I think I'll go and join in again, anyway, there's only ten
minutes left. Nine minutes . . . two minutes, finished.

Yawn, I am *sooo* tired, I'm going to bed straightaway.

Kathryn Sibley (12)
Forest Girls' School

A DAY IN THE LIFE OF A MIRROR

So here I am. My back flat against a wall as usual, watching my reflected world go by, oh, oh! Someone's coming over. It's a girl. She's trying on a pair of hideous shoes. They are luminous pink with a yellow frilly bow at the toe.

I suppose that's the worst part of being a mirror in Marks and Spencer's. However tragic a person may look, you're not allowed to tell them. If you did you would be blown up by the M&S Ministry of Magical Beings *(MOMB)*. This almost happened to me once. A girl was staring at me for *ages!* After about three hours, I was about to shout *'Take a picture, it lasts longer!'* when the girl stuck her tongue out. I was so surprised that it came out as *'Teeak'* I received a severe warning from *MOMB* for that indiscretion.

Then suddenly Miss Pink Shoes spoke, 'I don't care if you don't like what I'm wearing. I've only been staring into the mirror for so long because I like to take my time . . . plus I like to listen to other people's thoughts.'
'Do you have magical powers too?' I said.
'No,' she replied. 'But my name is Alice and I live in Wonderland.'

She said it so simply, as though talking to a mirror was part of her everyday life. Maybe it was.

It made me think though. Perhaps I'm not the only one with a secret life.

Rebecca Ball (11)
Forest Girls' School

A Day In The Life Of Gum!

Hi, I'm Wrigley's. Well, here I am sitting in my packet with all my other friends waiting to be bought. Ooh, here we go! Someone has picked us up. This person looks very young . . . a boy! Yuck! Boys' pockets normally reek! In we go, oh, his pocket seems nice, very fresh. Bump, bump, bump we go. All we seem to do is sit in people's pockets. he is picking me up now . . . he's opening the packet, it's me, it's me, he is taking me! *Gulp!*

Yuck, his breath smells like pickled onion. No wonder he needs us 'minty and fresh' gum. Looks like he has a few fillings too. The boy is walking towards a girl now and they begin to have a conversation. Chewing with your mouth open, very rude!

'Hi, Casey,' he says.
'All right Brad,' Casey says. So his name is Brad, very nice, shame it doesn't suit his breath!
'So,' Brad says as he looks down at his feet.
'So,' Casey whispers as she shrugs her shoulders.

Just after those words, I was about to experience the worst time of my five-and-a-half minute life . . .

Brad and Casey walked towards each other, they stretched out their arms and kissed! It was horrible, tongues moving and saliva spreading. It was *nasty!* But then something happened, I moved into Casey's mouth! Then she spat me out! Thump! There I was, on the dirty pavement with saliva holding me down, ready to be stepped on.

My life's over!

Elaine Antwi (12)
Forest Girls' School

A Day In The Life Of A Squirrel

Hi, I'm that really cute ball of fluff that crawls around in your garden and I climb those trees, the really tall ones, the ones you can hardly see the top of. Guessed yet? I'm a squirrel and I'm a pretty hungry squirrel too. You see, it's autumn and in autumn it's every squirrel for himself. Because everyone is scurrying around trying to get stocked up for winter. I've tried and I've worked so hard but my stock is emptier than usual. Wait a minute, I see nuts and big nuts too.

Mmm, these are pretty big ones. Maybe I should use these in my stock. There are loads and I'm beginning to think they're leading somewhere. What's that? Probably nothing. I thought I heard some rustling in the bushes. *Wham!*

Humans have captured me in a net and are dragging me away from my home and those scrumptious nuts, I can't wait till - no! I'm close to death and all I can think of is food.

I've been put in a dark, dim room in a tight-spaced cage doing nothing. Here comes a man carrying a key and wearing a white coat (how strange). He's picking me up and I'm out of the room. Aah! I think I've just died. This light is so bright! I can't see, this is just what wise old Jamala said it would be like. I can see again! I see a poster, it says 'For Vivisection'! *Aaahhh!*

Emma Bosch (12)
Forest Girls' School

A DAY IN THE LIFE OF AN INTELLIGENT BABY

'Put me down!' I think as a weird giant picks me up saying 'Who's a cute little rubbery dubbery then?'
What can she say about rubber dubbery? She has lots of rubbery dubbery jelly on her!

Monday, the worst day, because lots of jelly giants come over to our house. Mummy comes over and picks me up, carries me over the bumpy universe to my chair on stilts and puts me down with a jerk. Daddy then comes over to me, gives me worms with meat. My favourite! Mummy calls it Spaghetti Bolognese but I call it the 'Worm Special'.

Afterwards, all the jelly giants go into the playroom to look at the new wallpaper. It's been specially designed for my innocent-looking sister, Katy. All pink. All for her when she's a spoilt giant and pinches me all the time. I hate her.

Anyway, so all of these jelly giants are looking at the pink paper when suddenly Katy falls over. Don't you think that this is such a coincidence that every Monday after meal-time before presents are given out, she falls over? All of the other giants think this is innocent but I can see through her. She only does this so that the presents will be given out earlier as a medicine to make her feel better.

I am given a blue teddy with scary eyes as my present.

At seven I am put in my cot. I stare into the scary eyes of my new teddy, it is horrible! Who would give a baby a scary teddy?

I fall asleep gazing into its scary eyes.

Carmella Clarke (12)
Forest Girls' School

A DAY IN THE LIFE OF A CAT

I was rudely awoken up by my master snoring. I tried to wake him up by stamping all over him because I wanted my breakfast but I couldn't shift him. So I gave up and went downstairs.

I decided to wash myself thoroughly so I licked my paws where all the bits of dirt were and then I cleaned the rest of my body to make myself look beautiful. Head-first out the cat flap. I stumbled down the stairs into the garden. In the far end of the garden, I caught sight of a bird twittering away on the fence. Slowly, carefully, silently, I crept towards the distant fence. The bird was unaware of my approach.

When I was within range, I *leapt* through the air and . . . missed! The bird had seen me coming and had shot up into the air and soon disappeared into a neighbouring wood. Totally frustrated, I wandered around the garden patrolling the territory, checking there were no enemies lurking.

I came back up the steps to enter the kitchen. Once I was inside I could see there was food in my bowl; chunky rabbit and salmon in jelly, with tasty biscuits and a mound of grated cheese. I began to consume my meal.

Wearily, with a full stomach, I headed for my favourite comfortable spot on the sofa, where I curled up and went to sleep. In my dreams I was Lord of the garden and a vicious destroyer of all kinds of birds.

Katherine Turner (12)
Forest Girls' School

A DAY IN THE LIFE OF A BROTHER

I'm looking around the house; I don't know what to do. Should I go and play the PlayStation or should I go and play with my toys. I ask Mum for a lollipop, she says 'Yes.' I have my lollipop. I see my older sister talking on the phone to her friends (I will never do that when I'm older). I say,

'Who are you talking to?'

She says, 'Mind your own business and go and play with your toys.'

I come out of her room just as she asks and then I hear her say, 'That brother of mine is so annoying! He can never leave me alone in peace!'

I'll get her for that, I hardly ever get to see her all day because she goes to this Forest School place and when she comes in she goes straight to her homework which is just boring. She finally finishes off on the phone, I look at her and she looks at me, What are you looking at, shrimp?' she says.

'Nothing but a big ugly sister,' I say and I run for the stairs. Luckily she doesn't run but she tells Mum and I get told off. She looks pleased with herself and smirks at me (I'll get her for that as well). Then Mum says something terrible, every little boy's nightmare!

'We have to go shopping at Tesco's.'

'Tesco's!' I think.

Just then, I see my big sister smirk at me once more. She knows how I hate going to Tesco's (lucky for her they've got a clothes section in there).

After that I get to watch a movie. *Yesss!*

Varisse Colphon (12)
Forest Girls' School

A Day In The Life Of Queen Elizabeth

I wake up forgetting that I'm not a twelve-year-old girl who goes to school with her sister, I'm Elizabeth, not just plain Elizabeth but Queen Elizabeth. I decide to go and see my mother. I phone her first to see whether she is alright. She sounds very well and delighted to hear from me.

I arrive there in no time. I get out of the car and walk up to the front door. I pull my jacket down and check all the buttons are done up and I knock at the door. I hear some footsteps coming up from behind the front door. The door opens and I walk inside. As I walk around I admire the ornaments although I have seen them many times before. At the end of the hall I see my mother, I also recognise another face, it is my grandson, Harry.

I walk into the living room where I sit down and sip my cup of tea the maid brought. My mother starts asking questions and then the conversation starts changing into how much havoc her hip has been causing her. Then Harry starts talking. I look at my watch. I start to apologise and say that I have to leave. I walk to the car.

The journey home is also very quick and before I know it I am in bed. I start thinking about how quickly my life has gone and then I drift off into a sleep.

Caroline Wood (12)
Forest Girls' School

A DAY IN THE LIFE OF A BABY

I can be many things except a baby!

At first I thought, 'Yeah! Being a baby is going to be great, my parents waiting on me hand and foot, all the fuss over me, just me!'

But then I thought, 'All I'll do is drink milk, not be able to talk to anyone and worst of all, not be able to walk. Not be able to walk up the high road with my friends, uhm, am I sure I want to be a baby?'

My first day home! For the past two days of my life I've hardly been able to sleep, all those giants crowding round me, pinching my cheeks, looking at me like an extinct animal in a zoo.

I thought those days were over when I got home, but no, the minute I got home it started again. Why was all the fuss over me? Why not someone else? Why not my brother sulking in the corner playing with his big Lego bricks with which it looked as though he was trying to build a house? If only I could tell them to stop. I only wanted it to be my mum, my dad, my brother and me.

Although I was surrounded by people the whole time, I got so lonely, What could I do except drink, sleep, cry and get laughed at just because of my gummy lips sucking on my 'Whinnie the Pooh' dummy.

Yes! At last I could sleep and sink into my dreams while my mum sung 'Lullaby baby, the cradle will rock.' Then I was being pulled about by a giant calling herself 'Aunty Anne'!

Then I was asleep!

Next morning, I was twelve again.

Chloe Daltrey (12)
Forest Girls' School

A DAY IN THE LIFE OF A QUESTION

Hi, my name is Lucy Question. At school I am always asking questions like 'Why is a blackboard black?' 'Why is the sky blue?' 'Why is the grass green?' 'Why can birds fly and we cannot?' I love asking questions.

I ask them all day long, my friends say 'Can you please stop asking such silly questions, they are the silliest questions in the world, just stop asking questions!' But I do not care what they say, I love asking questions.

'Good morning class, I am your latest teacher. Please take out your maths book and turn to page 148. Lucy, open your maths book, do not daydream.'

Whoosh, boom, 'Where am I? I am supposed to be in maths.'
'Sit down.'
'What are you? How did you get here?'
'Hi, my name is Lucy, I do not know how I got here and I am supposed to be in maths. Where am I?'
'You are in a question.'
'How do I get out?'
'Guess! Good luck.'

Lucy walked around the question, she came to these voices, she asked them how to get out. Each one told her a direction to go. She found her way out in the very end by asking questions.

Motto: always ask questions.

Kathryn Court (12)
Forest Girls' School

A Day In The Life Of Claire

I wake up and then go and brush my teeth while trying to keep awake. After changing into my training kit I pack my lunch and then head off for training.

As I warm up I can feel the bitter weather pricking my skin. I line up with my friends, Susan and Emma, to start the race. The sun has just started to smile and bring a little warmth to the air. As I wait in anticipation to hear the gun crack, I can feel the sun shining on my back like a candle burning. Then, go . . .! I rush off like a fired bullet trying to defy the speed of sound. As I come close to the end my heart is saying well done! Well Done! Well done! As I cross the finishing line an enormous smile, as wide as the equator, appears on my face and the sun shines brightly to acknowledge my achievement.

As I drag my aching muscles home I remember the pile of homework that is waiting for me and my smile slowly disappears while my heart beats slower and slower.

Now instead of being immersed in joy I am engrossed in books. My head hurts from doing all the work and it still looks like I have loads left to do! My head and my hands feel heavy and they want to stop working but they can't. They know that if it is not done today then they will have even more work tomorrow.

As I brush my teeth for bed I think how lucky I am in being given the privilege to do athletics, especially as I am recuperating after the car crash two years ago, that left me in a wheelchair.

Katherine Bloomfield (12)
Forest Girls' School

A DAY IN THE LIFE OF A BULLY VICTIM

She was going to get me. I saw her long, wavy hair around the corner of the girls' toilets. The wind slapped my face like cold, wet hands. I thought this place would be a safe haven. A quiet refuge from the shouts and laughs. Her flashing blue eyes had spotted me. She walked towards me staring as though I was some animal in a zoo. I wished that Miss Huchet's voice would echo around the playground calling us for dinner, but no. Horrneta's voice rang out instead.

'Why does Mummy have to know about our little secret? It was lucky I came along when I did wasn't it?' She sneered pulling my hair and digging her sharp nails into my neck. My heart was pounding inside my chest so hard it felt like it was going to burst out. I felt a solitary tear roll down my cheek as she taunted me, whispering harshly into my ear telling me how she was going to make sure I didn't tell again. I felt defenceless, weak but under the fear and the hurt there was anger. Anger bubbling up inside me like I was a volcano about to erupt. As she started to shout and pinch me I felt she was eating away at my soul. 1 I felt cascades of tears pushing against my closed eyelids like an angry river pushing against a dam. I couldn't cry it would make things worse. But the sadness built up inside me made it impossible. Tears ran down my cheeks like a waterfall.

'*You!*' I sobbed. '*I hate you! You're just a bully and this is what I think of you!*' I was yelling, letting years of built up emotion break free as I spat at her feet laughing I felt free. I stood up to her and I'm so glad. I hope others do too.

Victoria Heasman (11)
Forest Girls' School

ELLEN MACARTHUR

Ellen Macarthur sets a great example to men and women all over the world, women in particular. She risked her life out on the ocean but in the end she succeeded and got exactly what she wanted, her dream came true and she didn't give up. Hers is one of many stories:-

Ellen woke early after only one hour's sleep, her boat was rocking fiercely and the heavy rain was falling on the boat. She got up and went to the deck, it was dark and most of the lights had gone out. Then suddenly she looked up to see the sail was going to rip, what could she do? What if she fell? What if this? What if that? Ellen had no time for doubts; she had to be brave and quick. She scrambled up the mast, fighting for her life. She had to be very tactful. She was amazingly brave and in the end she succeeded and she had managed to do it all by herself, in fact she had spent the whole journey by herself.

Ellen was lonely throughout her journey. She definitely inspires me and many other people. And I really think she is one of the most amazing new people I have ever heard of and it just goes to show that if you are really determined your dreams will come true.

Georgia Neve (12)
Forest Girls' School

A DAY IN THE LIFE OF FLORENCE NIGHTINGALE

I am woken early in the morning by crying. It is coming from a man writhing in pain in the furthest bed. His sheets are covered with blood stains. I am used to dealing with this situation as I am a nurse. *Bang!* Another cannon has been fired. At the moment I am in Turkey treating the wounded soldiers that are fighting in the Crimean War. Thirty-eight other women have joined me on this trip. Some are qualified nurses and others are caterers.

A man limps into the small, cramped room with an open wound to his leg. I fear that he may lose it and may no longer be able to fight. Incidents like these are quite regular.

The job is stressful and emotional. There are many people who I may not be able to help and this is quite upsetting, but I am starting to learn to keep myself optimistic about the futures of these young men. There are also many people who can be treated and soldiers who recover. It is an overwhelming moment when I see soldiers getting up and walking out the door to join the rest of the army in battle.

I work through the day and through the night, trying to accommodate the soldiers' needs. Sometimes, I have no sleep for several days.

Every evening I get out my lantern and walk around the hospital, checking to make sure these soldiers are as comfortable as possible.

Hannah Lamb (12)
Forest Girls' School

A Day In The Life Of Aaliyah (Romeo Must Die)

I woke up one sunny day, I looked at the time it was 7.00am. I slept in for two hours! I quickly brushed my teeth and I put my clothes on. I then did my hair. My limousine came and beeped. So I came out of my house whilst eating my toast. I jumped in the limousine. There was lots of traffic on the motorway. I heard these girls saying, 'Oh look, there is Aaliyah in the limousine, I can just about see her.' She was saying it to her friends in the car. They then said, 'Come on, let's ask for her autograph.' So they came and asked. My driver gave me one of his card signs saying 'No' on it, I put it against the window. I thought it was funny.

I finally got to the studio at last. Everyone was already there waiting for me. Jet Li was already ready. All the make-up artists and hair stylists were all over me. Everyone had to wait two hours for me. I then started doing the movie with Jet Li. This was our first day, we had got about two more months to go to complete the movie. I quite enjoyed the first day, but it took thirteen hours!

I had one of my cars at the studio, I drove to McDonald's to get some food, I was starving. When I was there the manager asked me for my autograph, so I gave it to him. They gave me food for free! I got home, ate my delicious food and watched the television for a bit and went to bed, *finally!*

Yen Pham (12)
Forest Girls' School

A Day In The Life Of A Siamese Twin, Aged Two

Today is the day. We walk together, co-ordinating our steps. I stumble and fall, pulling my brother down with me. Sammy and I are stuck together. I always have to face him. Mummy says we share a heart and the doctor is going to make us better today. We reach the stairs and struggle to get down them. Mummy sees us and comes running. She scoops us up and starts crying. Why is she so sad?

Sammy and I wander into our bedroom where Daddy is sitting, staring out the window. He's crying and when he sees us he stops and lifts us up, hugging us close. I can't breathe and I feel like screaming. But I don't because Daddy is crying and Daddy never cries.

We arrive at the hospital and get out. We wait for hours in a boring room with other people. They are shouting and a lady in white is trying to calm them. But when they see me and Sammy they stop and stare at us like we're aliens. Have we done something wrong?

The doctor sees us and feeds us a sweetie. Obediently, I chew it. I feel sleepy, but I need to tell Sammy something. He is already asleep. I'll tell him when I wake up.

I wake up to see Mummy and Daddy. They have tear-stained faces and smother me with hugs and shower me with kisses. But I try and push away. Where is Sammy? We are not together and I need to tell him something. I feel lonely as I realise, Sammy is gone and he's not coming back.

Hasreet Kaur (12)
Forest Girls' School

A DAY IN THE LIFE OF JENNIFER LOPEZ

A day in the life of Jennifer Lopez must be very hard work for she has to wake up very early every day and work, work, work! She must have a very busy and complicated life for she is a singer, dancer and actress. Jennifer has been very successful in all of these three things.

When she is filming, Jennifer must be at the studios by 6am. This means she can't have any late nights. At the end of the day, Jennifer might have an engagement in the evening, such as a film premiere or a recording session. She tries to lead a full social life too. As one of the world's most attractive women, she has had many male admirers including the notorious rap singer Puff Daddy.

Her life must be very demanding for she has to do concerts, films, recording and make videos for her songs and probably many more things. Jennifer has had two very successful albums and has made several excellent films.

Jennifer is a brilliant dancer for she does Latin American, Salsa, Hip-Hop and lots of other dance styles.

Jennifer is an inspiration to many young girls, including myself. She is a multi-talented artist who combines beauty with brains. Jennifer is very well known all over the world and I imagine that her parents are very proud of her achievements.

Cilpa Beechook (12)
Forest Girls' School

A DAY IN THE LIFE OF A SHOE

Oh no here she comes again with those smelly socks. I had finally got to sleep, but no, she would have to come along with her big, fat, size six feet and squeeze into me. No consideration for me and how I feel.

She started her usual walk up the hill. She suddenly came to a halt. She started leaning on my side. She does this all the time, she miss-shapes me and I become very fat.

I think she's waiting for a bus now, oh look here it is. She gets on the bus and she takes her feet out of me. What a relief. After a while she shoves her feet back into me and gets off the bus. Perfect, now she has gone and trod in bubble gum. It feels all sticky and every step she takes, more and more dirt sticks to me.

Oh great here comes the rain, it is going to wash the gum off me and make me wet and soggy!

As luck would have it, the sun comes out quite quickly. Good! This will help dry me off. She walks through the fields and to my disgust, she treads in dog's poo! I smell like I don't know what!

Finally she arrives home. She throws me into her bedroom and that is the end of my day.

I will have to do it all over again tomorrow and for the rest of my life!

Cordelia Gordon (12)
Forest Girls' School

A Day In The Life Of . . .

Even though I hated the baker and his family, I knew that they were inside and I didn't want them to be burnt alive. I ducked my head and leapt inside, avoiding the flames. Luckily, some were small enough to leap over. 'Is anyone here?' I called. No one answered. I felt despair grip my heart with its cold fingers, but I kept going. I flew up the stairs and reached the baker's living quarters. Then I saw them. They had been eating a meal and the baker and his wife had passed out.

Slapping their faces I shouted, 'Wake up!' Dozily the baker opened his eyes, 'W-what?' he asked in a voice blurred with sleep.
'The bakery is on fire!' I yelled.

Against the roar of the crackling flames, my voice sounded high and ethereal. By now tongues of fire were licking the door and the smoke was choking. The baker jumped up, lifted his fainted wife easily and sprinted down the burning stairs. I started to follow, but as he hurried, the stairs fell in. Then it struck me. The baker's daughter was still in the house! I ran desperately around the room. I opened the cupboard door and there she was! She was whimpering in fright. I carried her out. She was feather-light, but I was tired and couldn't hold her for long. I threw open a window. Levering the girl round to my back, I started to climb down. Cheers met me as I descended. The climb seemed interminable but finally I reached the ground.
'Are you OK' gasped the baker's wife, running towards me.
'I'm fine!' I replied. I took a small step forwards, then my ankle buckled and all went black.

Rachel Filar (12)
Forest Girls' School

A DAY IN THE LIFE OF . . .

Oh no, stop be careful! Blast it; I'm dirty yet again. Oh hi there, sorry, let me introduce myself. I'm Clogs and I'm a size five shoe, yes a talking shoe. Well I'd rather be you because my life is arduous.

I was born in a factory and dumped in a place called Barratts. Soon I was taken by my owner, Serena. She is a good owner but she likes stepping into dirt.

One day she was going to school she stepped onto a pin. Oh that hurt it was if somebody had poked me in the eye. Oh how that hurt, it took her two days for her to take it out. The same day she stepped in chewing gum, my worst enemy.

Anyway now we are walking down the street and . . . 98, 99, 100. Sorry I am now covered in 100 dead ants. Oh poo, what's that smell. Oh no! Oh no! Stop! Please! This is worse than my worst nightmare. Go on you can laugh you will never understand. I'm covered in dog doo. Knowing Serena she will clean me up, hopefully. I think the worst time of my life was when Serena enjoyed collecting pins in her shoe. How could she think of such a mean way to torture me.

Anyway I hope now you have read this you will treat shoes with better care, because we have lives too.

Koreta Findley (11)
Forest Girls' School

A Day In The Life Of A Credit Card

I am in my owner's purse, waiting to be used. I am a Platinum Visa Card. My limit is £10,000. My owner is a young lady. Through cash machines and into tills, buying things. From shoes to clothes to jewellery. My owner is pretty rich, by the look of it. It is so tiring being a credit card, after all that hard work. Here we go again, wait, that's not my owner, someone else is using me. I'm stolen! Help me.

It was a young man, he put me in his wallet. It was a dirty, torn up wallet. He looked like a robber to me. What was he doing? He was trying to take money from the checkpoint, but he didn't have the pin number, so he threw me away on the floor.

Out of a shop, opposite the pavement, a lady was crossing the road and it looked like my owner. She was going to go to a boutique which was in front of me.

Five minutes later, the lady came out from the boutique looking worried. She was probably looking for me. There was a bench next to me where I was and she sat there. She bent forward and there she saw the card that matched her description. Next she picked me up and realised that it was her card. She went back into the boutique and bought all she wanted and came out happy.

Amna Hussain Shaikh (12)
Forest Girls' School

A DAY IN THE LIFE OF . . .

It was cosy in my case, but Amy woke especially early to practise. I was angry at being disturbed and would not let Amy play nicely, which was a bad move, as she threw me on the floor, breaking my bridge. I can still feel the pain from it. I saw my friend Mr Bow lying next to me, over tightened, with many broken hairs.

I remember then being put back inside my case by Amy's mum and turfed into the boot of their car. We went bumping from side to side until the car finally stopped outside the Redbridge Music School, the place I've been so many times. I knew I would be handed to that man who hurts me even more than I already am, but thinks he's trying to help. Andrew, I think his name is.

At last Andrew had finished with me. I was handed over to Amy who took me into a weird room, where she played me until a tall man came and asked Amy to follow him. Amy followed Mr Blett (the tall man) into another room, where at one end a blonde woman was sitting behind a desk. Mr Blett also sat behind the table and listened as Amy played me. I had learnt my lesson about co-operating, so let Amy play very well. That was probably very wise, as when Amy came out of the room, I heard her mum ask, 'How was your violin exam Amy?'

Hester Klimach (12)
Forest Girls' School

A Day In The Life Of A Bully

There she was, Samantha Davis, sitting on the cold, lonely steps leading into the school. I think she thought she was safe from me there. She had started school last week and was small and feeble. I am stronger and larger, so Samantha made the perfect easy target.

I approached her. There weren't any teachers about. Samantha had long, flowing, blonde hair that fell onto her face. I began to jeer at her and pull at her hair.
'Stop! Stop!' she begged, as tears ran down her pale cheeks.
'Rapunzel, let down your hair! Are you waiting for the prince to rescue you, weakling?' I said in a mocking voice.

Then I started to pinch her. I demanded she give me all her money. As I was taking it, Mrs Lord was approaching us. I grabbed the money and ran off.

At lunch I found Samantha hidden in the shadows back at the steps. Her eyes were still bloodshot from her crying. I started pulling her hair again and taunting her.
'Stop it!' she stammered. 'I hate you! You like bullying people and hurting them just for fun. You're the weakling, just trying to act strong. I hope someone bullies you, so you know what it feels like!'

I stood there stunned at what she just said, as she ran off, tears streaming down her face. Later on in the day I thought about what Samantha had said. I realised she was right. I didn't understand how she felt before. At the end of school I saw her and apologised. I gave the money back to her and asked if we could be friends.

Kimberley Ng (12)
Forest Girls' School

A Day In The Life Of An Alien From Mars Who Is On Earth

I've just landed on Earth. I'm from Mars and my name is Yogootooo. It's 10am by the 'digital watch' on a human's paw. Things are very weird here. For breakfast, I saw someone eat something called a 'sandwich'. It's made of substances called 'bread, ham and butter'. I've signed up to go to 'school'. This is a place where you learn things. I want to go here to learn. Right now I'm on my way to this school place. Half an hour later I've learnt a lot of new words. I've made a dictionary and plan to make copies of it and sell them to other aliens on Mars. The dictionary doesn't have all the words that are spoken on Earth, but only the ones I've learnt. I tried some of the Earth's food but I don't like it. I like the food we have. We eat the insides of animals. It's yummy. They have these brown, round things on Earth. They are disgusting! I asked a person what these round brown things are and he said they were cakes. What a weird name. I'm flying back to Mars in my spaceship and I think I can see another spaceship. Oh no, I was mistaken, it's an aeroplane.

Daryna Menshova (11)
Forest Girls' School

A DAY IN THE LIFE OF A LOUSE

I started off on a dog this morning, but suddenly, the alarm went off to tell us that McBeth (the dog) was going to be sprayed! We all ran for cover but my family were too slow and got sprayed to death. Actually I was the only one who survived. I was devastated. All my friends and family gone, just because of one selfish human. So I decided to get my revenge. I jumped on her head. It just happened to be the head of Mary Mckenzie an English teacher at Forest School.

She rode her bike to Forest School, where she bumped into Mrs Lain, a sports teacher, but I didn't like the look of her hair. So I decided to build a house. It was quite a small house as there was only me living there. As the day went by I saw lots of other heads but none that tickled my fancy. It was the last lesson of the day and I had given up hope of finding another head, when suddenly I struck gold! I saw the head for me. She was an auburn and already had lice living on her head. Her name was Suzie. I packed my things and jumped. I nearly didn't make it but of course I did (otherwise I wouldn't be telling you this story). I made friends quite quickly and in no time I had a loving family and a big house.

Gemma Crozier (11)
Forest Girls' School

A DAY IN THE LIFE OF A CIGARETTE

I was fast asleep in my nice warm packet with my friends when suddenly I woke up. Colin, my best friend, whispered softly,
'The time has come.' I screamed. That woke everyone up. Colin continued,
'We are about to be bought. Brace yourselves.'

We sat upright in the box, jolting and bumping around, waiting for the horror of being lit, smoked and stumped out. We went into a handbag and the very fat lady waddled towards the bus stop. In the handbag were some disgusting things. Yuck! A dirty old tissue. It stinks in here. Ouch! We've just been dumped onto a table. Oh no! She's taking us out. Opening the packet, lifting me up, I can't move. There's the lighter. Arghh! My bum! It kills! I'm almost gone.

Wheee! That was the most fun I've ever had. Better than being in that stuffy packet. Uh? It's all gone dark. *Splat!* That was me; I was stepped on.

I lay there in bits, for about half an hour until that dreaded street cleaner came. Phew! He missed. I'm being stepped on every second now. Oh no, I can feel my life going, going, gone! I've been stepped on one too many times.

Lucy Boggis (12)
Forest Girls' School

A DAY IN THE LIFE OF A 50P

Hi, I'm sure we must've met before. I'll give you a clue as to what I am.
I'm made of metal. I'm small and extremely useful. Get it? I'm a 50p.
Let me tell you about my life . . .

I'm usually stuffed into a purse. No one thinks about how I must feel,
all squashed and crowded. Life in a purse or wallet is *very*
uncomfortable! After being in there for what seems like years, I'm
finally taken out. I'm then exchanged for something with a shopkeeper,
usually sweets! Next I'm put into a till, still a bit crowded but better
than being in a pocket and hey, I'm with my friends. But before long a
hand comes in and yet again I'm on another journey.

Let me tell you about my worst experience . . .
I was put in a game machine in an arcade but as usual before long, I was
taken out and cashed into the bank for £10 notes. How unfair! I was left
in a bag in a horrible cold box. I was in there for ages. But then I
escaped, I was free, free to be spent. Life as a 50p can be quite
interesting, but tiring. One day I'll be forgotten, no use. I hate that
thought, me, no use! What a load of rubbish! Oh wait, someone's
picking me up. I've got to go, but remember, every time you use a 50p
treat it nicely, we have feelings as well!

Sophie Fraser (12)
Forest Girls' School

A DAY IN THE LIFE OF 50P

I'm going to give you two clues about what I am. I have the queen's head on one side and Britannia on the other and two is that I'm a hexagon shape. Can you guess yet? To save your brains racking so much I'll just tell you, I'm a fifty pence.

My life is a new adventure nearly every day because I always end up in a different purse or shop, but my most exciting story would have to be when I ended up in a safe.

This day began with a young girl called Kate (well I think her name was Kate). Her mum had given me to Kate as her pocket money and Kate put me in her purse and she set off for the sweet shop.

Kate's hand reached in her purse and light started to fill the purse. Her fingers were coming towards me and oh! Oh! She's picked me up. Kate gave me to the shopkeeper and he shut me in the till where there was no light at all. The only light I saw for the rest of the day was when the till kept opening and more coins were being put in. By the end of the day the till was packed with lots of coins. The man emptied us all out of the till and put us in a bag, then took us to the safe and then locked us in there for ages. This was my last adventure.

Kellie Holland (11)
Forest Girls' School

A DAY IN THE LIFE OF A FOUNTAIN PEN

I felt lucky today. I was very excited. I couldn't wait for someone to buy me just so that I could feel loved. I was at the front of the shelf and a pretty little girl picked me up, she turned me upside down and I felt sick. She was squeezing me whilst I was still in the packet. I couldn't believe that she took me to the counter. I had never before seen this blue surface. She handed me over to the lady behind the counter who zapped me and the number, 4.99 appeared on the screen. 4.99, what does that mean? Aaahhh she threw me into a bag. Wow it's like a white cocoon in here. I can just see out, I think this is going to be a bumpy ride. Ouch! She dropped me, she should be more careful.

After a while she put me on a hard, cold table. She picked me up. It's cold outside of the bag. Aaahhh she's ripped off my packet and thrown it on the floor - what a litter bug. She's taken off my lid and unscrewed my top. I hate being taken apart. Oh no, she can't get the cartridge in. Someone else is trying now, it just won't work. I am being taken back to the shop. I am a bit disappointed but at least I can see my old mates again. I can tell them that life's better in here. The outside world is scary.

Emma Winders (12)
Forest Girls' School

A DAY IN THE LIFE OF A CRISP WRAPPER

I am living in the dark tunnel. It can be so frightening. I will tell you how I got here. Let's start at the beginning.

The strangest thing happened. This young girl came into the shop and picked me up. She squeezed me tight as she walked to the counter in the shop. I had seen this happen many times but didn't realise how scary it was. As I left the shop, I couldn't see a thing. They had encased me in a plastic material. Everything went dark. The milk carton next to me was sending a chill through my exterior. Next thing I knew this pink hand was coming towards me and coiled its fingers around me. It pulled me out of the material and prised open my head. Slowly the young girl ate away my insides. As she finished, she stood up and just dropped me. I slowly fluttered to the ground.

All these people keep walking past me. One man was walking along, kicking a can. Oh no! It's Cindy! The can is Cindy, one of my closest friends. She left the shop days ago. Then there was this old man. He was carrying a pointed stick and whistling. He stared down, then the spike went right through me and lifted me high into the air, letting go over a dark hole. I fell onto piles of rubbish. This is how I came to be living in a tunnel. At least it was exciting.

Ruby Penny (12)
Forest Girls' School

A DAY IN THE LIFE OF A RAINDROP

I am a small particle of water being tossed around in the turbulent seas of the Indian Ocean. Suddenly, the sun emerges from behind a cloud, the temperature rises dramatically. I can feel myself rising and fragmenting into water vapour.

Swiftly ascending into the sky, the temperature drops and I fuse with my fellow droplets to form a cumulus cloud. It is shaped like a dragon with fiery breath! We gather speed as the wind picks up and pushes us westwards over Africa. Some of my friends break from the cloud and fall as rain onto the safari plains of Kenya. I survive.

We scud over the Atlantic Ocean towards our goal. I am destined to fall over the tropical rainforests of Costa Rica.

I expand into a huge raindrop and the fury of the torrential downpour explodes.

Oh, here I go, falling, falling towards the canopy of trees below. As I hurtle downwards I am breaking into many smaller drops.

The sun miraculously appears and as the sunlight enters my world, it bends and reflects, forming a beautiful rainbow exhibiting all seven colours of the spectrum. The spectacular rainbow arches into a flowing ribbon of colour.

I continue to race downwards to the forest floor. It's getting closer and I brace myself for the heavy impact.

Bump! I hit the ground with such force I shatter into smithereens and give up my life to the soil so that plants may flourish.

Nicola Wolstenholme (12)
Forest Girls' School

A DAY IN THE LIFE OF DENNIS BERGKAMP

'Run, run, run, up, run , run, run, up.'
Training, eating, going to sleep and in a match. Interesting! When I was younger this was the life that I wanted. My older brother told me that it would be girls, girls and more girls, instead it is more like eat, sleep and breathe football! I am scared of flying in planes so when I go somewhere for a match I have to go on ferries or cruise ships.

Ahhh! Someone help me to break this cycle of work.

Do not get me wrong, Arsenal is an amazing side to play for and I am privileged to be a part of it *but* surely there is more to life than this; I have fans, managers and money.

Maybe I could:
Become a Buddha.
Maybe I could give everything away to charity.
Maybe I could live in a third world country.

Maybe the true meaning of life, I would have to search for . . .

'Dennis, wake up! Are you in dreamland?'

Carly Moore-Martin (12)
Forest Girls' School

A Day In The Life Of A Bear

Hi! I am Buffy the bear and this is my story about how I got here.

It all started at the home of the bears - 'Build-a-Bear'. This is where I sat for about two months feeling sad and lonely, when all of a sudden I was picked up.

'I want this one!' shouted a little girl, who was only about three years old.
'OK then' said an old woman. 'Let's go!'

She took me to the 'fluff 'n' puff' machine. This was where the Build-a-Bear staff worked. One of them put a long cold tube into my back and then filled me with a mixture of fluff, feathers and beans. I was getting fatter and fatter by the second. But then, when I felt I would burst - it stopped.

The little girl, whose name was Morgan, picked a heart out of a box, made a wish and then put it inside me. I started to feel it beating - really fast. I was then taken for my first bath - which was called an air bath. Morgan put her foot on the pedal and a puff of cold air made me shiver. But afterwards my fur felt much better. I was then taken to be registered and was given my birth certificate.

I was then taken home to Morgan's house, where I met all the other bears. That was the start of my adventures!

Lauren McKellar (12)
Forest Girls' School

A Day In The Life Of Elvis

He woke up peaceful and calm with his wife Priscilla. He got dressed and went out, but then his face fell. He heard all the fans shouting for his autograph.

Then he got bored with writing all of them. When he got to the stadium he had butterflies in his stomach. But he heard his name being called out by the compere. He came out and he was burning hot with all the smoke.
The crowd was shouting and he was singing 'You're Nothing But A Hound Dog.'

Then the compere said that he was going to sing 'Blue Suede Shoes' which was a very early song from the 70's. He went home very happy.

Ben Eggleton (8)
HAMPSTEAD HILL SCHOOL

A Day In The Life Of Russell Crowe

Russell Crowe was resting from a shoot, when his director said
'Come on you'll be Maximus, you'll be stabbed.' So Maximus got
hung. They added a little bit of make-up. Caesar read his script and
lightly stabbed him (fatally though).

Then he got sent into the arena. He pretended that he was weak. He had
armour on him and they fought each other. Caesar was winning but then
he dropped his sword. He asked his men to throw him a sword but they
didn't because they saw what he had done to Maximus. But Maximus
dropped his sword and they started fighting with their hands and
Maximus won.

Serioja Kohli (8)
Hampstead Hill School

A Day In The Life Of Galileo Galilei

In one day Galileo Galilei changed the way we look at the world and the galaxies. He found that by putting a convex and a concave lens together in a tube, which we now call the optical tube, he could make faraway objects look much nearer. He had invented the telescope!

His first telescope magnified things by only three times. By experimenting he came up with one that could magnify by sixty times.

Using this telescope he proved that all the planets move around the sun, not the other way 'round. He also did something that would not only make him blind, but would make a major discovery. He found little black spots on the sun which we now know are flares as big as the Earth.

Twenty-four years after his invention of the telescope, Galileo got put into prison because he disagreed with the Church. But now we know that Galileo was right.

Sam MacKinnon (7)
Hampstead Hill School

A DAY IN THE LIFE OF ALEXANDER FLEMING

I, Alexander Fleming was eating a sandwich. I was looking at the Typhus Bacterium, a dangerous bacteria that carries typhoid. My mate scientist then shouted something. I dropped my sandwich and ran into his lab. He said he had discovered a new element.

'How many electrons and protons?'

'112 electrons and 112 protons.'

'Which makes its atomic mass 224.'

'So what do you call it?'

'Unalbinium'

I thought that was the biggest breakthrough the hospital was going to have, until I looked through the microscope. I saw a mould I had left in the sandwich had dripped onto the germs and killed them.

I shall call this *penicillin!* The saviour of hundreds of lives.

I am a rich man now. My name will go down in history.

Gabriel Turner (8)
Hampstead Hill School

A DAY IN THE LIFE OF CHUCK JONES

Chuck Jones woke up in his house and had some toast. He got in his car and drove to his studio. He was making a new cartoon called 'Prisoners in Space'. He drew it out. Daffy Duck was blowing up Bugs Bunny but his beak blew sideways and fell off.

Afterwards the duck fell off a cliff and the rabbit met a hunter. The hunter also fell off the cliff and squashed Daffy Duck. When he got to the end it was an hour long. The cartoon was finished. He went home and prepared for his next cartoon.

Mischa Frankl-Duval (7)
Hampstead Hill School

A Day In The Life Of Picasso

One day Picasso went to the wild wood, it was a lovely sunny day. He started sketching a sleeping owl. Then he sketched a frog which had yellow skin. He sketched the famous rubber tree plant. Next he sketched the Hawaiian dancing lizard.

As you know Picasso is a Spanish artist so his pictures are amazing. He lay down quietly and sketched a flock of birds by the name of blackbirds. Next he went to the Spanish coast and sketched starfish, a few crabs and a cuttlefish.

He was exhausted and walked home.

Fred Isaac (7)
Hampstead Hill School

A DAY IN THE LIFE OF WALT DISNEY

One day Walt Disney was in his studio drawing Donald Duck. He had just finished it when it moved. He thought he was imagining it.

Then he started drawing Pluto. When he had finished the drawing wagged its tail. 'This is the paper that fell out of the sky, it could be magic.' said Walt Disney to himself. He was a bit scared.

He carried on. He started colouring. When he had finished colouring Pluto, Pluto jumped out of the picture. Walt Disney fainted. The police were walking past the studio and heard a dog barking. The police were tempted to go in. He nearly fainted when he saw Pluto chasing a cat and the cat trying to get the fish and Walt Disney had fainted. He grabbed Pluto and left the cat with the fish. He saw the picture with Donald moving.

He grabbed that up as well and had not time to faint. When he got out of the studio he thought Pluto came from the piece of paper. He stuffed Pluto into the paper and tore the paper into pieces before Pluto could come out again. As for Walt Disney, he went straight to hospital. As for the fish, it had been gobbled up by the cat!

Oliver Freedman (8)
Hampstead Hill School

A Day In The Life Of Blackbeard, The Pirate

Blackbeard was one of the most fearsome pirates. His real name was Edward Teach but his private name was Blackbeard because he grew his beard much longer than any ordinary man and it was black.

Blackbeard was on the poop deck, steering the ship. Then there was a shout 'Ship Ho!'
'Where are we Redhand?' shouted Blackbeard.
'Due Northwest' shouted back Redhand.
'Right then, all hands on deck, sail Northwest. We have a Spanish ship in our hands.' shouted Blackbeard and some others. So they sailed and sailed till they were side to side with a ship. As the Spanish ship was hardly armed, Blackbeard's men shot cannons and threw grappling hooks. The Spanish ship was captured very quickly. Blackbeard and his men were rewarded with 10,000 gold pieces. Blackbeard was a very skilled pirate.

Jobi Tan (8)
Hampstead Hill School

A DAY IN THE LIFE OF A TURTLE

Dear Humans

I am a turtle called Tia. I live in the Pacific Ocean. Once a year, the beach I live on in Zanzibar, looks as if it's been patrolled by army tanks overnight because of the marks in the sand. But no, these are not tank marks but turtle tracks. These are of turtles coming ashore to lay their eggs. This is the biggest event of the year.

I'm a female turtle which means I'm one of those poor things that has to lug their heavy shells up the beach to the right nesting areas. We lay about 100 eggs at a time, in hole that we've scooped out with our flippers. Then we cover the hole with sand and do the hard journey back to the sea.

Let me tell you a bit more about me and last year's journey. Last year I lost 50 babies. You see, what happened is, about nine weeks after I'd laid my eggs they hatched. (That happens with all turtles' babies) They hatch on their own without me being around so they have to fend for themselves. That day, half of my year's greatest event was ruined by seagulls.

Morning

I did the struggle up the beach, using my flippers to push the sand away to form a hole when I got to the top.

Evening

I experienced the pain of my eggs pushing out. Then I struggled back down the beach and slid into the ocean for nine weeks.

Evening

When my turtles hatched they had the longest journey of all for their small flippers. The seagulls nipped them and scratched them until 50 of my poor babies died. I don't know where the rest are.

Anyway, the rest of my life is fun. I swim, eat seaweed and play with my turtle friends.

Tia T.

Madeleine Hill (11)
Lauriston Primary School

A DAY IN THE LIFE OF A WARTHOG

When I get up in the morning I turn over another side of my calendar and then go and wake my mum and dad. When I have woken them up I ask them if I am allowed to go and grub for berries from the forest for my breakfast.

After I have eaten I ask my mum if I can go and play with my friends that live in the neighbouring bush. Most of my friends live right next door to me. But a few of them live very far away so I can only communicate with them by smell that travels through the air. I am very lucky because I am able to be a parent when I am only one and a half years old.

By now it's about midday and I start to get hungry. My parents go out to boar Bingo, so what I have for lunch is entirely up to me. When I do actually eat my lunch I can eat as much as I want and I usually eat until I have to puke, (sort of like a buffet). When I have eaten I play a couple of games with my mum. Then my mum forces me to do my drum practice, when I bang on the trunk of a tree. Then I have to go to bed because I get up very early in the morning.

Stephen Thompson (11)
Lauriston Primary School

A DAY IN THE LIFE OF A BUTTERFLY

As I struggled out of my pupa, I saw sunlight for the very first time in four weeks. I have been transformed into a butterfly! I was a caterpillar but ever since I've been inside my pupa something magical happened. I want to know how we caterpillars change into butterflies? I know we change inside a pupa, but I can't see how. Did God just make us like that or do we just change into them naturally? I wonder if I could ask Him and get an answer . . . or not?

As I stepped through the afternoon, I started to wonder If I could fly around the world . . . or not? It's silly really because I keep on asking myself all these silly questions. I know, I can go and see if I can find any nice flowers to rest on. That might stop me from talking to myself. It doesn't really work. I'm still talking to myself. I just wish that I could just be normal like my mum and dad were. I mean, they got kidnapped and they are in a butterfly farm being treated like dirt and I don't know how they are doing in there. I would love to know! The thing is, they could be dead. Oh why am I thinking such horrible thoughts?

It's nearly the evening and I'm thinking about my parents. I think I'll just leave it and stop thinking about it. Maybe if I go to sleep, then I'll forget about it tomorrow. Then I'll see what adventures I might have!

Lucy Johnson (10)
Lauriston Primary School

UNTITLED

Dear Diary

I woke up this morning and had a nice juicy cricket . . . only normal. I spent my day up in the trees, seeing as I'm a tree frog. I looked for a tree where I could blend in perfectly. When I found the tree I picked a neat, flat leaf and the sharpest, smoothest twig I could find and began to scratch this neat poem about myself.

I'm green all over
I have a white underbelly
I'm a white tree frog
And I feel like jelly.

I live in Australia
Shaded in a tree
Camouflaged by leaves
So you can't see.

After writing my poems, I usually play a game. One of my favourites is 'Hide but still see'. It goes like this. Find a hunting animal near a large tree, hide in the tree, making sure you can see the animal. Jump in front of the animal and them jump back up the tree. Do this daring sport till the animal starts to grow angry. Many a time I've been chased but I've never been caught. Sometimes I wish I could be colourful like my cousins but I couldn't play my game then could I, because I'd be seen too easily? Anyway, my cousins are poisonous.

Anyhow, I spent my evening with Mrs Jelly Belly in the home tree. Just us two croaking about the day and eating soft, moist crickets.

Mr Jelly Belly.

Lauren Belcher (10)
Lauriston Primary School

A Day In The Life Of Sir Alex Ferguson

Plan:

Manchester United gets Mr Ferguson as a manager, and they win the first match 14 - 1.

Ferguson scared to leave United

Ferguson decides to go to Liverpool and then everybody moans at Alex.

I have been put under pressure by the French Club. B Levers needed to leave the club. The fans want me to go to Manchester United because they need a manager to boost them up to the high level, like the world of Brazilian football. The FA had a meeting about whether I should be going to United or not. They requested that it would cost over £100,000 pounds for B Levers to sell me.

When the crisis was on the news, everybody went mad, even I was surprised. I had to have an interview with Sky News 24, John Kayso asked me whether I wanted to leave my present club, I responded madly at the newsreader 'Why won't I leave B Leverson . . . to go and manage Manchester United for them to turn out to be the best club in the world. If the FA wanted me to move, I think I would prefer going to Liverpool.'

When I got in my BMW to drive to my stylish cottage in Scotland, I spun round and yelled madly 'The FA's finally made a decision!'
So you can see that this day in my life was chaos.

Javed Moore (10)
Lauriston Primary School

UNTITLED

'Where am I?' I said, feeling lost and dizzy.

One minute I was climbing a tree now I'm face down in bubbly mud.
I pushed myself up with my paws. Paws wait I was just a normal human
now, now . . . I'm a flying squirrel 'Kraa, kraa!'

I heard someone or something shout, I turned around and saw a massive
crow flying towards me. I dropped down on my four paws and ran for
my life. I reached a ditch, I felt a tickle of fear flow through my small
body. I leapt high in the air attempting to jump over the ditch when
something grabbed my back legs and pulled me into the ditch.

'Are you out of your mind?' a gruff voice said.

I looked up, it was a ginger flying squirrel. I started to feel embarrassed
because there were lots of other squirrels next to him staring at me
angrily.

'Anyway, enough of that we've got more important things to worry
about, I got a message from our cousins the bats, the crows are coming
for our food again.' said a male squirrel who was standing next to the
ginger squirrel. In less than a split second, a massive hollow log rolled
down into the ditch, out from the log crawled a mousy-grey squirrel.

'Well come and get your armour and weapons then,' he said in a
squeaky voice.

Everyone ran into the tree trunk, so I followed them.
Everyone was picking up weapons and armour.

I took some silver leg armour and a breastplate. I went outside and
started getting the armour on. As I placed my helmet on and strapped
my belt on, I remembered how evil the crow was that had tried to attack
me, and they were the creatures we were about to fight.

When all the squirrels joined me, we climbed out of the ditch only to be met by about thirty crows. The squirrels were already throwing stones and nuts at them. Twelve of the squirrels ran away and a crow flew up to us and was greeted by a stick being cracked on its head. There were screams of agony emanating from the crow's mouth. Seventeen of the crows flew away and then there was only one crow left. I threw a stone at its head and it flew away.

The battle was won.

Johnny Adair (10)
Lauriston Primary School

FAMILIES

Families are so much fun
they share and care when you are there
they give you buns
and they also brush your hair.

They are lovely and beautiful
they help you when you are ill
they are so wonderful
and they also pay the bill!

They love you
they're always there
they always say *'You're so cute!'*
and look after you when you need the care.

Meera Patel (11)
Leopold Primary School

A DAY IN THE LIFE OF A WHALE

Whale . . .
More liquid than the water
through which you move.
As you perform your tricks
'How do you feel?'
Fluent fluid swimmer
With muscles like blue-grey steel
You seem to laugh and smile.
Have you heard the rumour
That you're the only broad big-tailed mammal
With wide sensitive eyes?
In the depths of the sea you're a king
What do you think of the fishermen
Who catch you for your oily skin and blubber?
Does the clear water wipe whale's whimpering?
As you sense other defenceless whales
Rescuing whales from tight, horrible fishermen's nets.

Reiss Tibby (11)
Leopold Primary School

AN ASTRONAUT'S DIARY

I am Astronaut Pearl

Sunday 12th June 2000.

First day of training, I was very nervous. I thought I was going to die.
I felt the weightlessness going down my body as I was floating.
We all had to do it, it was practise repairing satellites.

Monday 13th June 2000

Today I have learned about how to escape from the emergency exits in
the space shuttle. It was very exciting, I was almost ready to go into
space.

Tuesday 14th June 2000

Today I am on the spacecraft and the food is horrible, I was sick four
times, I don't think I can eat anymore.

Wednesday 15th June 2000

Sally and I went out to fix the Satellite. Sally went first and suddenly
her tube snapped. Luckily there was a rope nearby and I pulled her in.
Sally was safe again.

Thursday 16th June 2000

After the excitement , we were finally able to fix the Satellite. It was
nearly time to go back to Earth.

Friday 17th June 2000

A letter to my mum

Dear mum

I am writing to tell you about the wonderful time we've had in space. It
was exciting and the view was beautiful. I wish you were here.
From your loving dearest daughter

Pearl.

Saturday 18th June 2000

We arrived back on Earth and I thought that I could write a book about my time in space all about the excitement and the beauty and the feelings you get.

Pearl Kooyoo Filson (11)
Leopold Primary School

BIGGEST BUSINESS WOMAN

Not many people know this person but she is a big hit. Maybe not world famous nor the richest in the world, but this woman is very dear to me and is very successful.

Mrs U M Agbasimelo is a very successful business woman who works and specialises in the field of marketing.

She said goodbye to her husband and two children Chiso, Charles, Kene Agbasimelo as she was leaving the house. 'Goodbye' they called after her.

That was the last thing she heard as she was leaving the house.

'Goodbye!'

She entered her car and is driven to work by her driver.
Mrs Agbasimelo arrives at her office that day to find out that they were to do an advertisement for their number one product 'Tenderly' and guess who was the star - Mrs Agbasimelo herself. She was a star shining in the night sky, her smile was an encouragement. Straight away she got to work and they started to build on the idea.

She worked and strived hard but one thing she cannot fail in, is her faith in the Lord.

'Can I take five please Director?' she asked.
'Yes you can!'
'God bless you!'

She goes off on her way, she had been trying to make the baby they were using happy for three hours!

She calls home to tell them the good news.
'This is so good,' she says 'you don't know how happy I am!'
After her break she goes back to work.

After her work has been finished she gets back into the car to be driven back home - she reaches home tired but still an air of achievement fills the atmosphere.

Mrs U M Agbasimelo is a heroine - my heroine because I would like to be her and follow in her footsteps.

Chiso Agbasimelo (10)
Leopold Primary School

FOOTBALL SPEAKS OUT

The game is about to begin, they put me down in the middle and when they put me down I get anxious, nervous and even tense.

I know when they're going to kick me. Oh poor me, I'm only a football.

When the referee blows the whistle, I try not to tense up even more, they kick me about up and down. Hard, soft and all sorts. Oh poor me, I'm only a football.

When I go into the net, one team is cheering and the other team is sad not saying a word, wishing I was in their net and I say put me down gently. Oh, poor me, I'm only a football.

No, they throw me far and the crowd cheers when I'm up in the air,, heading for their net, being passed around. Oh, poor me, I'm only a football.

One of the players headed me into the net and they cheered with so much joy the other players.
No goal!
Oh, poor me, I'm only a football.

But at the end of the day they blessed me and Beckham took me home. Washed me and put me in a glass cabinet. Oh, yes I'm a football.

Ever since then Beckham and his son took me out and played with me, doing skills, then washed me spotlessly clean and put me back in my new home.

Oh yes, I'm a football . . . Football.

Erica Blackwood (10)
Leopold Primary School

THE NEW NIKE SHOES

In Stonebridge there is a new shoe factory just opened. There are three hundred workers in the factory.

One worker cuts my leather the other worker stitches me together. Another worker polishes me and other workers make my Nike logo and another colours my Nike logo in shiny gold. Then I am put in an beautiful elegant box with white coloured tissue paper which I call my nice comfortable bed.

When I am finished I am transported by a lorry with my brothers and sisters. I arrive at 2pm with my brothers and sisters.

As soon as I got in the shop, the shopkeeper takes me out of my nice bed which humans call a box and he puts me on the shelf gently. It was a Saturday morning and the shops are open. I woke up with joy, people were looking at me through the window with happiness on their faces.

Then a boy came into the shop looking at me and smiling. He put his foot inside me and his feet smelled of cheese and his feet could not fit into me properly.

Next, a beautiful girl picked me up to try me on. I knew she was the right one because she had a Nike dress on. She slipped her feet into me and I wiggled so that her foot could be comfortable.

She was happy and her mum said 'Do you like them?'
'Yes!' she replied
Her mum got her purse out and gave the shopkeeper £30.00 and she walked out with excitement.

Bianca Polius (11)
Leopold Primary School

SHOES SPEAK OUT

I am a high heeled shoe
a very high one indeed
I was shipped from America
to London's Shoe Express.
Placed on the top shelf
showing off my beauty
to the people.

I am the best out of all the others
everyone loves me.
This little girl who is a princess
came in and she loved me.
She asked her dad if she could buy me
her dad said 'yes'.
She was happy when he did.

She tried me on
We fitted perfectly.
Next, she took me to the counter
and paid for me.
I cost ninety pounds.
I know she'll take care of me,
and I was really happy.

She wore me to church
to parties here and there.
Even at her school she runs everywhere,
she loves me a lot, she cares for me too.
I always get cleaned up and polished
But I know one day she will get tired of me
and pass me on to her little sister.

I hope she will be like my first owner
but I wish that she would give me away
because she is the only owner I have had so far.
I have had the best time with my owner.

Shanika Lamoth (11)
Leopold Primary School

IF PICTURES COULD SPEAK

It was a beautiful sunny Thursday morning when something strange happened to me. I will tell you this strange story if you won't tell anybody else.

That Thursday morning my class was going on a school trip to an exhibition of paintings. When we got there I was so bored with looking at the lifeless paintings, I wanted something exciting to happen, but I didn't know if it would come true.

Finally I saw something I liked. Hanging in front of me was a 'World War 2' picture. This one was for me, it was of a famous soldier with the name Peter de Mort. As I looked around the rest of my friends had gone, in fact there was no one around, I was all alone. As I ran to catch up with the rest of them . . . a voice called me back.

'Wait, don't go and leave me here!'

I looked around, there was no one there, then as I moved closer, I saw the lips of the picture move as it spoke again.

'Please don't leave me, talk to me for a while!'

As I turned back slowly, I thought to myself a picture talking? I closed my eyes hoping I would wake up in my bed. I smacked my face, but this was no dream I was in. Then the picture spoke again.

'Stay and have a chat with me boy!'

I went and stood up in front of the picture. I found out that after just about twenty minutes that I had so much in common with the painting and I wanted to show him to some of my friends.

I took them back to the painting but it never said a single word.

Then we had to leave for school, but when I turned and looked over at my soldier, he winked.

Then I had an amazing idea.

After school I went home and drew my own picture and named him, so I had a friend wherever I went.

That is why today we can't tell anybody about the pictures seen as they still live on.

Ramone Russell-Rhoden (11)
Leopold Primary School

The Call Up

It was the 3rd of July. Today was my birthday. I woke up feeling lucky. I had a bath and I made myself a special birthday breakfast. I was just about to meet my friend Tricia when the phone rang. Oh! I thought as I went back to pick it up.

'Hello, is this Natasha Phillips?' Asked a familiar voice.
'Yes it is' I replied.
'I am ringing to tell you that you're going to be on 'Who Wants To Be A Millionaire'. We will be expecting you on Tuesday 9th July. When you come in, give us a list of your phone a friend's numbers.' He explained.

After I put the phone down, I started to shake with an excited feeling. I couldn't believe who the call was from.

I rushed down to Costa Coffee in Brent Cross to tell Tricia the great news.

'Congratulations, birthday girl!' she cried.
She was so happy for me. I still couldn't believe it myself. Tricia and I went on a shopping spree. We visited nearly all of the shops, then Tricia asked me 'What are you going to wear?'
'I haven't the foggiest!' I replied.
So we spent some more time looking for a dress. I finally found a dress which cost me £75.

Tricia and I went to my apartment, I tried on my new dress and we sat at the table and made a list of phone a friend numbers. We had a meal then I phoned my family telling them the great news. They were all happy for me and they congratulated me. Tricia stayed at my house that night. I got into bed. 'This is the most thrilling birthday ever. No words can ever describe the way I am feeling.' I thought luckily. I fell asleep.

I awoke the next day, I went to work and I asked all the people I had listed if they would all be home on that night. They all assured me that they would. I had squared it with my boss and promised to work overtime.

Days passed rapidly. All I could think about was 'Who Wants To Be A Millionaire'. Then the day finally came.

I woke up at 5 o'clock in the morning. I felt refreshed and had a nice cold shower and a special breakfast. The doorbell rang. It was Tricia 'I've come to wish you good luck,' she said 'I've brought this along', she said as she held up a silver necklace.
'I can't take this!' I exclaimed. 'It's your lucky locket.'
'Take it!' she said.
Then I went to Elstree Studios.

I dropped off my list of phone a friend to the telephonist's office. I met Chris Tarrant 'We'll be on air in one minute!' He told me. 'Good luck,' he said in a warm, comfortable voice.

'In 10 9 8 . . .1 and action!' The director shouted. The audience applauded.

Mr Tarrant said the fastest finger, first question.
I knew the answer straight away, when I had finished I crossed my fingers.
'Only one person got it right and that is Natasha Phillips in 2.62 seconds' he announced.

The audience gave a round of applause. He explained the rules and I started to play the game.

I answered the questions with confidence I was on £500,000 but I was stuck on the next question. I had used all my other lifelines up except 'phone a friend' earlier on in the game.

I phoned Tricia, she said she was 65% sure the answer was Claude Monet. I began to think *what if she's wrong?* Will I be able to forgive her? I went with her answer, my heart began to beat rapidly

'Natasha, Natasha!' Chris called slyly.
'You have just won £1,000,000!'

I jumped for joy, I couldn't believe it, he placed the cheque in my hand.

> Who Wants To Be A Millionaire?
> To: Natasha Phillips
> The sum of £1,000.000
>   Chris Tarrant.

That was the best feeling I could ever have. I gave Tricia £16,000 for helping me.

I still have to work overtime though!

Grace Oyesoro (10)
Leopold Primary School

A Day In The Life Of A Superstar

Glitz and glamour,
Sparkles and fun.
Hollywood hotels,
Sand, sea and sun.

Tons of work, piling up
You have no time,
To sit and sup.

A superstar's work is never done
It can't all be fun, fun, fun;
I try my hardest, I try my best,
It's still not enough to pass the test.

The salary's boombastic,
But not everything's fantastic.
For instance, the boss nags me all the time:
'Nausheen, hurry up. You're on in nine!'

It's worthwhile in the end
When I see my fans,
Cheering and screaming
And moving their hands.

Whether I'm singing, dancing, acting or presenting,
I always do my best,
And with every bit of stress,
I feel twice as much of a success.

So now you see a day in the life of a superstar
Is not exactly as easy as can be,
It has its ups, it has its downs,
But for now I'm going to be back to being me!

Nausheen Ali Subhan (11)
Leopold Primary School

WHERE AM I?

It was a Monday morning and I was another year older because it was my birthday and I felt terrible. I had a nasty headache which had started yesterday.

When I went downstairs, my breakfast was already made, lying on the table. My mum, dad and little sister were all being nice to me when my dad gave me a gift in an envelope. I opened it and looked down, it was two tickets to go and see 'Lil Bow Wow' live in concert. I gave my dad a big hug and said 'How did you get these?'
He happily said 'I won them on the radio.'

I phoned my friend Kim to tell her we could both go and see 'Lil Bow Wow' in France. She was so excited, she asked 'When is it?'
'Next week . . . Saturday' I replied.

The week went by as fast as a cheetah and my clothes were packed. It was going to be the best sixteenth birthday party especially when there were no adults coming.

We were off on the train, ready to travel over the English Channel to get there. We arrived somewhere, definitely not France, because every thing looked different I could not recognise anything that I had seen before when I had visited this town in France.

I asked 'Where am I?'

It was a foreign country, people were wearing different types of clothes and funny looking red hats and the place was crowded like a swarm of bees and everything looked blurred.

We went to the security guard (who could not even speak English) he was absolutely useless. So we went back to the train station to find someone and we found a tall elegant woman who worked there; we asked her 'When is the next train back to England please?'
She replied 'In five minutes.'
But we only had the money for one train ticket, so one of us had to hide.

The train came, our tactics would have to work, it was our only chance to get back home but it didn't work. The ticket collector found out and he asked us to get off the train.

We were so upset that we started to cry, but luckily there was another man who was a God-send. He said 'I have two tickets for England because my daughter and I were leaving today, but we have decided to stay in Italy for a while longer, so it would be a waste of tickets and you can have them.'

'Italy!' we shouted
'Thank you!'

So we took the train back home and everything was alright even though we did not get to see 'Lil Bow Wow'. We were still safe at home with our family. But we now know that it's not always safe to go without an adult.

Ebony Douglas (11)
Leopold Primary School

THE DAY IN THE LIFE OF MY DOG LADY

The day in the life of my dog lady
Everyone surrounded by the baby . . .
I wonder what she's thinking,
Really I do!
Does she want to play around?
I really wonder, honestly I do . . .

Then off she goes for her breakfast,
What would it be today
Chunky chicken or maybe fish meats.
I wonder what she would like
Really I do?

Or would she prefer chicken tuna . . .
Oh dear, how I would love to know.
Then off she goes to dig a hole
Playing with the soil as if it was a doll.

As the day comes to an end
The garden is left for me to mend!

Nicole Renwick (10)
Leopold Primary School

FUN FAIR

It was a special day for Ashley.

It was the middle of half-term and she decided that today instead of staying at home she would go out and have some fun. The only trouble was she did not know what to do.

She started to read the newspaper when she noticed a big bold colourful advert which read 'Funfair'.

'Yahoo!' she shouted jumping up and down.

Very soon she realised that she would not be able to go because she didn't have any money. She went upstairs and tipped her money box upside down but nothing came out. She sat on her bed and tried to think of a plan, she went outside and did things that got her money. Like walk dogs, wash cars and plenty of other things.

She went and knocked for Holly, and her friend Leanne. They got there and all three of them hopped onto the roller coaster. They were swerving and swinging and sliding everywhere. They got off laughing and joking around because they'd had so much fun. Next they went on the Helter-skelter they slid all the way down, swishing and swooshing down on a mat. Soon they got hungry and had a burger and a glass of lemonade.

Leanne hurt herself on the bumper-cars and Holly fell over and grazed her knee. Ashley was having a great time but had to go because Holly and Leanne had to go.

Then they caught the bus and went home. It was one of the greatest days they'd had and they had fun.

Ashley Beckford (10)
Montem Primary School

A DAY IN THE LIFE OF A DOG

One day I wasn't feeling in the mood to go anywhere, so I had an extra sleep and felt relaxed.

Felix my dog came into my bedroom and jumped on my bed at 4.30am and woke me up. I knew what she wanted, but I couldn't be bothered.

I ended up taking her for a walk and I met my friend Amerea, she was taking her dog Brooklyn for a walk also. We started to talk about shopping and asked each other do you fancy going clothes shopping? So we took our dogs home and I met her at her house.

We went to all the shops you could name and I was exhausted, so we both went to the café and had a muffin and tea to build up our strength. Now it was time to say goodbye to each other and says we'll keep in touch by phoning. The time was now 8.30pm and I went home and Felix was sleeping, so I put on the TV and was watching Eastenders. However I decided to phone Amerea and see what she was up to. She said 'Brooklyn is asleep and I'm watching Eastenders.'

She asked me 'Do you fancy going to the cinema to see 'The Mummy Returns'.

I responded with 'What time and when?'
She said to me 'Saturday, 12 00am.'

Zoe Ellis (11)
St Augustine's Primary School

A Day In The Life Of A Popstar

One fine sunny day I woke up, got up out of bed at 10.30am. I sat down on my sofa and said to myself 'I'm not going anywhere so I can relax.'

I looked up at the time and it was 10.55am I had only five minutes left and I ran into the bathroom and had a quick shower. I ran into my bedroom and I couldn't find anything to wear. When I had found something to wear I ran out of the house leaving my shoes behind. I ran back into the house to get my shoes and then ran to the car to meet my mum at the park.

When I reached the park I saw her sitting on the swings swinging back and forth. She jumped into my car and we were off to the Chinese shop. My mum bought some fried rice and spicy chicken and I had fried rice with sweet and sour chicken and we put it in a bag and went back to the park to eat it. When we had finished eating, we went to play for a little while and I forgot the time.

Because I didn't have my watch, I forgot about the time and went home. I didn't even go in I just met my friends who I was singing with and they jumped into my car and we went together. We sang well together and then it was home time. So we all went home and I went straight to bed.

PS: Remember tomorrow is another day.

Tiffany Hillman (11)
St Augustine's Primary School

A DAY IN THE LIFE OF TONY BLAIR

Trriiinnnggg! Oh the alarm, the alarm. Why does it have to ring when it's not wanted? I feel as if I've just crawled into bed. Why I wanted to become Prime Minister I don't know.

Well, just lying in bed isn't going to do me any good. Hup, two, three four . . . Into the bathroom, wash my teeth, into the bath tub and out I come. All the time I get dressed in a rush.

At 6.05am, I'm ready and settled at the dining table with my (secret) notebook, making notes about what I am going to be doing today. I make all sorts of notes, I write what I do each day. I write what I say to voters and everything.

Lunchtime. the word lunch is supposed to mean a big break from all the work you're doing, right? *Wrong!* For me it means more work, more thinking, more planning and more writing. My lunch is a small hurried meal (well kind of a meal anyway) with millions of black words on thousands of white papers.

Got to keep on going, got to keep on going. I have to chant that phrase every time I'm working to keep me working. You know I'm surprised that I don't wear glasses all the time, with all this reading I have to do. Very soon my right hand will wear away because I am writing so much.

An hour later, I head off to St Augustine's Primary School to talk to the teachers and pupils. I get there in 20 minutes. I am 10 minutes early for the meeting, so I am able to have a quick couple of biscuits and a cup of coffee.

At 1.30 the meeting starts with all the questions and answers. I tell them that I will make the taxes less and give them more school equipment such as rulers, pencils, rubbers, coloured pencils, computers and I will pay for all they need to buy for the school for three years.

Later at home:

I didn't like the children at St Augustine's, they were so horrible, they hardly paid attention to what I was saying. It was as if they saw right through me.

I have to go to bed at 10pm each night so that I can get at least 7 hours of sleep. I would sleep for at least a week if I could.

Fumbi Essiet (11)
St Augustine's Primary School

A DAY IN THE LIFE OF A POP STAR

6 o'clock in the morning and it's time to wake up.

I woke up and I was tired but hungry. I went down the stairs and gave a big yawn. I took some milk out of the fridge and got a glass. After breakfast I went down to have my wash but my friend Cherry was in there, so I read a book for a little while. I went in for a bath and when I got out the phone rang it was the dancing team to tell us that they are coming round in half an hour. I looked in the wardrobe and picked out an outfit that I felt comfortable in.

11 o'clock and the dance team came to pick us up.

It took around an hour to get there. We were in a big school hall where we were going to set the scene where we were singing. It was hard work, we had to sing the words and dance at the same time. After we went for lunch in a special food bar. We all talked about how far our song will get in the charts. After that we had to get ready for a quick concert in France.

10 o'clock in the evening and we're getting ready for the concert.

10 o'clock in the evening and we had to go to another concert in Newport where we were going to have a famous singing artist. He was going to the Brit Awards, we were going to show our new single to America for the first time. Before we went on the stage I had a big pile of butterflies in my belly. At 11 o'clock it was our time to go and perform our song for the first time.

At the end of the performance everybody clapped. I felt happy because it was all over. After the Brits it was 12.30pm and I was very tired.

Jordanne Williams (10)
St Augustine's Primary School

A DAY IN THE LIFE OF A POP STAR

When I got up in the morning, from 6am to 8am I had a long relaxing bath so that I smelt reasonable for when I rehearsed. For 8am to 10am I had a two hour feast of Fruitibix so that I didn't get hungry before 1pm. I wouldn't be eating lunch till 2pm.

At lunchtime my band and I met up for lunch till 3pm, but I didn't know that I would be eating at 12pm! I had chips, baked beans, scrambled eggs and a cup of coffee with my other pop star mates.

Then at 3pm I went to the BBC TV Centre in Shepherd's bush. From Shepherd's Bush I went to the stadium centre to rehearse my song. It's a hard life. Then I had to make brief notes for the big day.

I dropped off at my friend's for a bit of teacake and a cup of cappuccino.

Then the time it was 9pm, time had flown! My feelings were happy, I was thinking that if I do my pop star songs I would be paid a grand.

At home I said to my self I had had an important day, signing documents, being paid fees and more.

Lathaniel Dyer (10)
St Augustine's Primary School

A DAY IN THE LIFE OF A MEERKAT

Hi!

I'm Chelsea and I'm a meerkat. I'm going to tell you what happens in a day in the life of a meerkat.

Time to get up, it's 6am. I don't really want to get up, but I'm on guard duty. Up I go, searching for any predators.
'Hurry up, Sally,' I yell.
Sally and I are guards for that day.

We are standing there and nothing is coming. It gets to 8am and everyone is up. some males help us to keep a look out. All my friends are playing as we're still young, and all the older meerkats want a tan (or so they say.)

It gets to about 12pm so the older and wiser females go hunting (they're not really wise, just old!) I am sitting there daydreaming about what they will bring back.

Crack! We all stand up. It is a wolf running in. All the incredibly young children run in. We are going to battle the wolf. He comes closer, we keep still like a statue. He sniffs us. We bend our knees, and pounce right on him, He shakes his head. He is in a panic. The females come running back. They drop the food and bite him. He is running and running. He can't feel his way as we cover his eyes. I turn around to see all the young ones poking out. He runs, we jump off.

Yum! Yum! My wish comes true, we have rabbit. It isn't normal rabbit, it's fresh desert rabbit. I have enjoyed our battle. I go to get the young ones out. They are playing a game. I get them out and sit them with the rest.

We have just finished our dinner and I am lying down. I am so tired. I have been up since 6am for look out. I have to lie down to let my food digest. The little ones can run as soon as they finish. Well, they don't eat that much anyway.

I am all right now. I want to play with my friends. We have to look after the little ones so we play baby games. We want to play hide and seek but they're so easy to find and when they're 'it' they end up in tears because they can't find anyone.

Laura Reynolds (11)
St Augustine's Primary School

A Day In The Life Of A Cat

Today is a new day and I feel like I should sleep a little longer, say until 10am. The only reason I sleep so late is that I have meetings at night with my fellow cats and chase mice about. I think I'm good at that, yeah.

For lunch, well, I get Whiskas, but I prefer juicy mice. I go around climbing walls after lunch and when I get tired I lie on my basket and watch 'Cats are the next best thing.'

During the day I don't really do anything interesting so I just wander about the house. Well I suppose chasing mice is pretty interesting (if you're a cat).

I think the main thing I do is have cat meetings once a week. They're pretty interesting. I mean with all the discussion and democracy, it is interesting.

After chasing mice I go to take a nap on the sofa, then I purr a little. My owner is loving and she gives me food everyday and when I say a lot, I mean a lot.

She is much taller than me and unlike the other kid, she cares for me. She gives me rides and cleans out my basket. The boy is very ugly and he is a disappointment to the family.

Before bedtime, I go out again and look for mice. The mice that I find have to be juicy and tasty. If they are not, I don't bother with them.

The second best food I like is a can of Whiskas and a delicious bowl of milk. Mice, however, have to be the main dish.

Then, of course, on some nights I have to get my own food, say, go out and fish in the lake and get some fish and share 'em with my cat buddies.

I also know other important cat Members of Parliament and we have a quick chat with them to see what things have to change in the cat society. Considering I'm one of the main cats in the business, I have to attend these meetings.

I go partying with my family. Every time I mess about, so I have to be careful. Well that's about the whole of my day. Oh, and I come home very late, Usually at about 3am.

Rajesh Sagar (11)
St Augustine's Primary School

A Day In The Life Of A Mouse

One day in a small house on the edge of Greenville, lived a mouse (that's me) and a cat called Biscuit.

Every day I would get up early and wait till Anne (Biscuit's mum) would go out.

I had been dreaming of this day for a long, long time. As Anne walked out of the door, I ran and ran and ran till I came to the trap! The trap was the only thing that could stop me from getting the cheese. Luckily I had brought a stick to help me get the cheese. Then the cat jumped out of nowhere and ran after me. I ran and ran but he was still running after me, so I ran under a chair. After a minute or so, I sneaked out from under the chair and ran as fast as I could. Finally he wasn't running after me.
'Yes!' I thought, ' I have run too fast for him!'

At last I was right in front of the cheese. With the stick, I knocked the cheese off the mousetrap and ran home. Outside my door was the cat! I ran and ran. When I got him away from the door, I ran in.

When I got in, I was out of breath. Just before I got into bed, I ate my cheese. It was lovely.

Katrin Souter (10)
St Augustine's Primary School

A DAY IN THE LIFE OF A POP STAR

I wake up early this morning, again! Well I think it's early. My manager says it's late to wake up at 9 o'clock. I have such a wonderful life. The things that are wonderful, that I have done, are meeting the Queen, the President, the Prime Minister, Richard Blackwood, Little Kim and Mel B.

I manage to eat an apple, then the phone rings,
'Hi, is that Zil? It's Live and Kicking. Your manager told us you have a new song, and we wanted to ask if you would come on the show to perform your new single.'
'Yes!'

That afternoon I had lunch with Sian Kaywood because the Rugrats were on. We talked about shoes and all the rest of the girls' stuff. After lunch Kay (Sian) and I ran down to the studio. I was just in time to perform my new song, 'Party'. It was great! The crowd loved me, it was such great fun. I went to bed early that night, did I say early? I mean I was going to watch 'Die Hard' and after that, fall asleep in the chair.

Louise Thompson (10)
St Augustine's Primary School

A Day In The Life Of A Hamster

Up early again and still no food. I am very bored again and my owners are the most repulsive people in the whole world.

'Where is that no-good old cat?'

'Tiger, what are you doing?'

'Listen, I've got a plan. When our owners have gone to work, come and let me out of my cage and then we can get some food.'

'Yes, master, whatever you say.'

'Finally, they've gone. Tiger, go up to the window and check they're leaving.'

'Yes, they've gone, master.'

'All right, then, let me out of my cage.

'It is already 12pm. Go and get me some cheese and get whatever you want. I'll be on the sofa kicking back.'

In case you haven't guessed already, I'm a hamster, but unlike popular belief, the reality of the cat and hamster relationship is that we, the hamsters, are in charge! Yep, it's true.

'Thank you, Tiger. Come, let's watch TV. Turn it on.'

'Yes Your Highness.'

Munch, munch, munch. That was so lovely and my belly is very full now and there is a wicked show on MTV. I am not bored anymore and I am really enjoying this song, *'Get your groove on, get your groove on, go, go, go.'*

Tiger is very scared of my pointed teeth.

'Tiger, give my a piece of your hair so that I can floss my teeth.'

I watch him torture himself just to pluck a piece of his hair out.

Moments later

'They're back! Quick, pick up all that food and stuff it under the sofa, and turn off the TV. Then start to chase me, but don't hurt me.'

Door opens.
'Owww, get the cat off the hamster and boot the cat out.'

Back in the cage again, but there will be another day.

Romano Green (11)
St Augustine's Primary School

A DAY IN THE LIFE OF A HAMSTER

Up early and still no food waiting for me. Where is that good-for-nothing cat?

'Jessy, get your no-good old carcass over here and get me some food.'

'Yes, my great hamster. I am here to serve you.'

Stupid cat, it's soooo dumb, getting me food when I should be his food! I hope he doesn't just bring me some sunflower seeds or peanuts.

'I am back and brought you some seeds.'

'Seeds! You went all that way and you just brought back seeds? I should throw this back in your face, but I am hungry.'

'Look hamster, they're leaving. It's time . . . *to party!'*

'Quick, get the food and I'll break out. Don't forget to bring the nacho cheese. Now let's kick back and watch TV.'

Moments later

'They're back! Quick, try and clean up this mess now!'

'Yes my great hamster.'

(Door opens)

'Quick, pretend to hit me and I will fall on the ground. Ouch!'

That cat is so thick. Doesn't he know that if he hurts me he will get kicked out of the house?'

'Jessy, what on earth are you doing to the poor old hamster?'

Ha, ha, ha, never trust a hamster. Aah! Poor old cat.

Daryll McLeod (11)
St Augustine's Primary School

A DAY IN THE LIFE OF JEZIL THE ELF

Jezil the friendly little green elf woke up in a very cheerful way. He hopped into his crooked little cottage. Last night he had peacefully slept outdoors gazing into the breathtaking stars. He gobbled down a few of his yummy rock cakes, taking little breaks to have a sip of his tasty raspberry juice. He had made his sweet juice out of the juicy berries he had happily picked yesterday in the middle of his adventurous walk through the forest. Now Jezil's little tummy was absolutely full of yummy rock cakes and delicious raspberry juice. Jezil had a terrific idea. He was going to visit his best friend, Corey the unicorn. Corey and Jezil always played together happily. Jezil loved sunny summer. He and his friend would pop over to the bottomless lake and splash each other with cool water. He stumbled out of his little cottage delightedly thinking of fun things he and his friend could do. He hopped along to a path full of tiny pebbles. He finally reached his friend's house. They instantly decided to go to the cool lake where they would splash each other and slide from the gushing waterfall. In no time they were there. Jezil and Corey slid down the waterfall with extreme power, but they didn't land in gushing water, but a fresh green meadow with goblins, leprechauns, dragons, lions, fairies and warlocks. Jezil and Corey gasped. They couldn't believe their eyes, They crept around and popped their heads out of corners. Soon after everyone became the best of friends. Every single day they would go to this enchanting land and play games of tag for hours and hours.

Eleanor O'Driscoll (9)
St John Vianney RC Primary School

SCRAPS' DANGEROUS MISSION

There was once a mouse called Scraps who though small, was extremely determined and one day he announced at breakfast that it was time the small baggy mouse moved on and was going on an adventure, a mission, a challenge. He would meet a *dragon*. But little did he know of the difficulties to follow. He got a hanky he had found on a dirty human street, a thimble to use as a cup, tissue for a bed, a single pea and six breadcrumbs. Then late one winter evening he set off. It was raining hard and he was being hit on the head by giant boulders he didn't know were raindrops. then he ducked as a huge wet blue thing fell upon him.

'Oh no, the sky is falling. I will climb the mountain to the dragon's hut immediately.'

He set off on his dangerous mission to the top of the everlasting mountain. He climbed with an occasional stumble as he met a rock too big to leap. After several hours of impossible work he collapsed. When he woke, he shut his eyes against the frightful light. The sun was considering getting up from bed to give some light. Then a loud, unfamiliar voice made his blood run cold and he opened a nervous eye. It was the most amazing sight that Scraps had ever laid his small black beady eyes on. There was nothing he was used to on the dirty streets of London like broken glass or chip wrappers. There were no feet kicking him, no salesmen shooing him away. His first thought was that he was in Heaven. But as there was no sign of God, he looked around more closely. There were fields and fields of sweet green grass and beautiful flowers of all colours. Then in the distance he caught a glimpse of an emerald green hut with gold lettering saying *Dragon*. He dashed faster than a bullet, five more yards, four more yards. What if he blows me up? Three yards to go. What if he's moved house? Two more yards? What if he's hungry. *He was there!* With one trembling hand he pushed the door open. He clamped his eyes shut.

A deafening roar made his flesh creep and the hair on the back of his neck stand on end. He slowly opened one trembling eye and gave an ear-piercing scream. Not one, but seven enormous, scaly, fierce-looking dragons were standing side by side.

As it happened, the dragons did not blow him up. Also they were not hungry and then there he was on top of the mountain with a house labelled *Dragon* and a house labelled *Mouse.*

And Scraps lay down to sleep.

Kirsty Morrissey (9)
St John Vianney RC Primary School

A Day In The Life Of A Balloon

It was an ordinary multi-coloured balloon. One chubby man blew the balloon up until it was as fat as a ball. It was for a special occasion, at a party. The sparkling balloon could fly up high like a bird. Then one scorching, bright day, a rather short person let go of a magnificent bunch of balloons. As soon as it was up in the clear blue sky, the balloon went to an amazing, special place. It went to a place that no ordinary people go, only special and important people go there and do you know where it flew off to? Well, let me tell you where it went. It went to the Queen's palace in the garden. It was very green and it had a beautiful maze, fresh red roses and fountains, and there's so much more, I just could go on and on and on. After a while, the balloon was getting smaller and smaller until it could no longer exist. Then it floated back down to the ground, then it shrivelled up and lay there until someone threw it into the stinky dustbin and it was no longer seen again.

And that's the life of an ordinary balloon.

Alina Colaco (9)
St John Vianney RC Primary School